"THIS SEASON'S SLEEPER . . . BUT YOU SURE WON'T
SLEEP THROUGH IT. *NUTS* IS AN EXCITING SHOW!"
— *Associated Press*

"NUTS is simply terrific, old-time, belt them in the aisles, the
guts, and if necessary the kidneys theatre. Not only does it
have the audience rooting for the good guys and hating the bad
guys, as if the whole event was the most beautifully professional
wrestling match you have ever seen, NUTS is a play that moves
you. . . . The play deals with very serious questions—its
heroine, Claudia, is quite a lady with quite a problem. . . . The
situation is fascinating, and Tom Topor develops it with
uncanny skill. . . . With this one, unless you are some kind of
blue-blooded, weak-kneed and thoroughly rotten snob, you
are going to have a great time."
— Clive Barnes, *New York Post*

"A cross between *One Flew Over the Cuckoo's Nest* and *Whose
Life Is It Anyway?* . . . a salvo of emotional tracer bullets
that riddle hypocrisy."   — *Newsweek*

"Despite every temptation to go off its dramatic rocker, it resists
the temptation. . . . The tension builds and holds, without
overplaying. . . . NUTS is a wonderfully sane play."
— *San Francisco Chronicle*

TOM TOPOR was a newspaperman for twenty years, in
New York and Europe. He has published three novels, most
recently *Coda*, and is currently working on two screenplays
and a new novel.

NUTS

A Play in Three Acts

Tom Topor

A PLUME BOOK

NEW AMERICAN LIBRARY

NEW YORK AND SCARBOROUGH, ONTARIO

CAUTION: Professionals and amateurs are hereby warned that NUTS is subject to a royalty. It is fully protected under the copyright laws of the United States of America, the British Commonwealth, including Canada, and all other countries of the Copyright Union. All rights, including professional, amateur, motion pictures, recitation, lecturing, public reading, radio broadcasting, television, and the rights of translation into foreign languages are strictly reserved. In its present form the play is dedicated to the reading public only.

NUTS may be given stage presentation by amateurs upon payment of a royalty of Fifty Dollars for the first performance, and Forty Dollars for each additional performance, payable one week before the date when the play is given, to Samuel French, Inc., at 25 West 45th Street, New York, N. Y. 10036, or at 7623 Sunset Boulevard, Hollywood, Calif. 90046, or to Samuel French (Canada), Ltd., 80 Richmond Street East, Toronto, Ontario, Canada M5C 1P1.

Royalty of the required amount must be paid whether the play is presented for charity or gain and whether or not admission is charged.

Stock royalty quoted on application to Samuel French, Inc.

For all other rights than those stipulated above, apply to Lester Lewis Associates, Inc., 156 East 52nd St., New York, N. Y. 10022.

Particular emphasis is laid on the question of amateur or professional readings, permission and terms for which must be secured in writing from Samuel French, Inc.

Copying from this book in whole or in part is strictly forbidden by law, and the right of performance is not transferable.

Whenever the play is produced the following notice must appear on all programs, printing and advertising for the play: "Produced by special arrangement with Samuel French, Inc."

Due authorship credit must be given on all programs, printing and advertising for the play.

Anyone presenting the play shall not commit or authorize any act or omission by which the copyright of the play or the right to copyright same may be impaired.
No changes shall be made in the play for the purpose of your production unless authorized in writing.
The publication of this play does not imply that it is necessarily available for performance by amateurs or professionals. Amateurs and professionals considering a production are strongly advised in their own interests to apply to Samuel French, Inc., for consent before starting rehearsals, advertising, or booking a theatre or hall.

 PLUME TRADEMARK REG. U.S. PAT. OFF. AND FOREIGN COUNTRIES
REGISTERED TRADEMARK—MARCA REGISTRADA
HECHO EN BRATTLEBORO, VT., U.S.A.

SIGNET, SIGNET CLASSIC, MENTOR, ONYX, PLUME, MERIDIAN AND NAL BOOKS
are published *in the United States* by NAL PENGUIN INC.,
1633 Broadway, New York, New York 10019,
in Canada by The New American Library of Canada Limited,
81 Mack Avenue, Scarborough, Ontario M1L 1M8

Library of Congress Cataloging-in Publication Data

Topor, Tom, 1938–
  Nuts, a play in three acts.

  I. Title
[PS3570.065N8   1986]   812'.54   86-12609
ISBN 0-452-25872-3

First Plume Printing, November, 1986

2 3 4 5 6 7 8 9 10

PRINTED IN THE UNITED STATES OF AMERICA

Nuts, by Tom Topor; directed by Stephen Zuckerman; settings by Tom Schwinn; lighting by Roger Morgen; costumes by Christina Weppner; production stage manager, Lola Shumlin. The WPA Theater Production, Kyle Renick, producing director; presented by Stevie Phillips, in association with Universal Pictures; opened at the Biltmore Theatre, 261 West 47th Street, on April 28, 1980.

OFFICER HARRY HAGGERTY	*Dave Florek*
AARON LEVINSKY	*Richard Zobel*
FRANKLIN MACMILLAN	*Gregory Abels*
THE RECORDER	*Linda Howes*
ROSE KIRK	*Lenka Peterson*
ARTHUR KIRK	*Hansford Rowe*
DR. HERBERT ROSENTHAL	*Paul Stolarsky*
JUDGE MURDOCH	*Ed Van Nuys*
CLAUDIA FAITH DRAPER	*Anne Twomey*

Danny Kreitzberg and Bonnie Champion,
Associate Producers

NUTS

Act One

The courtroom in the psychiatric wing of Bellevue Hospital. It is just before 10 on a Tuesday morning in winter. Bright sunlight streams through the 3 windows on Stage Left. Up Stage Center is the bench—traditional, as is the raised witness stand to the left of the bench. In front of the bench is a small chair for the COURT RECORDER. *Up Left of the Bench is the* JUDGE'S *door—to the right are double doors leading to the outside corridor. Down Stage of the windows is a railing in front of which is the Defense Table with two chairs. One is between the table and the railing, this is the Defense Lawyer's chair, the other is on the Up Stage end of the table, this is the Defendant's chair. Just Up Stage of the Defendant's chair, Down Stage of the middle window, is the Court Officer's chair. On Stage Right is another railing extending from the doors all the way Down Stage. Against this railing are four chairs for the witnesses. In front of the witness chairs is another table. There is one chair at this table for the Prosecutor which is situated between the witness chairs and the table. Both tables are small and rectangular. The chairs are oak and armless except for the witness chairs and the chair on the witness stand. The judge's chair, behind the bench, is a high backed, executive chair. Stage Left of the judge's chair is the State flag of New York, to the right the flag of the United States. There are venetian blinds on all three windows, which are down but the slats are open. On the defense table is a pitcher of water with two glasses, on the prosecutor's table is a pitcher with one glass, and on the judge's bench is also a pitcher and one glass. This is what the audience sees as it comes in. The Curtain is never used during the show. The play begins with the lights going out.*

As the lights come back up, a bit brighter, the COURT OFFICER, HARRY HAGGERTY, *enters thru the Judge's door, Up Stage, Left of the bench. He crosses to the bench and lays some folders on it. He then crosses Left, stepping down from the witness stand and places a Bible on the window sill by his chair. He crosses to the Stage Right door and opens it.* AARON LEVINSKY *enters and crosses Down to the Prosecution table.* HARRY *goes to him and signals he's at the wrong table. As* LEVINSKY *crosses to Left of the defense table,* HARRY *crosses Up of the witness stand and turns on a light switch which lights up the two neon panels hanging above the set in Center Stage. The room is now filled with bright light.* HARRY *then crosses to the windows and closes the blinds.* LEVINSKY, *at his table, is taking his notepads out of his briefcase and laying them on the table.* FRANKLIN MACMILLAN *enters and crosses to the prosecution table.*

MACMILLAN: (*As he begins to empty his briefcase.*) Harry, how are you?

HARRY: Not bad.

MACMILLAN: (*Taking off his watch and putting it on the table.*) I hope he's not late. I have to be at the Appellate Division by noon.
(*The* RECORDER *comes in and crosses to her seat and begins to set up her machine.*)
Who's the judge?

HARRY: Murdoch.

MACMILLAN: Murdoch, huh?

(*To* LEVINSKY.) A Republican. But smart.
(LEVINSKY *smiles.* HARRY *exits thru Judge's door.*)
Article seven-thirties are a pain in the ass.
(*Pause.* LEVINSKY *sits.*)
You handle them much?

LEVINSKY: No. First time for me.

MACMILLAN: (*Glancing through his notes.*) Have you been on this case since the arraignment?

LEVINSKY: I joined the case later on—Aaron Levinsky—you should find a copy of the client's letter in your files.
(MACMILLAN *crosses to Center.* LEVINSKY *crosses to his Left.*)

MACMILLAN: Frank Macmillan.
(*They shake hands.*)
Do you do much criminal work, Mr. Levinsky?

LEVINSKY: More than enough to suit me.

MACMILLAN: I don't envy you this one—say, can she handle sitting through this; I've seen them crack wide open, and it's a bitch.

LEVINSKY: My fingers are crossed.

MACMILLAN: The thing about a case like this is you know it's cruel to prosecute and you know you can't leave her loose, you follow what I'm saying?

LEVINSKY: Hmmmmmmmm.
(ROSE *and* ARTHUR KIRK *enter. Both are in their 50's and prosperous looking. Like many people who aren't used to a courtroom, they are slightly overdressed, almost Sunday clothes.* ROSE, *in a fur jacket, and knit suit and pearls;* ARTHUR *in a formal suit, cashmere overcoat, hat in hand. They stand Up Right Center looking around. Finally* ARTHUR *clears his throat.*)

3

MACMILLAN: (*Turning and crosses Right of Center to greet them.*) Mr. and Mrs. Kirk?
(ARTHUR *nods.*)
I'm Frank Macmillan, from the district attorney's office. We spoke on the phone.
(*They shake hands with him.*)
This is Mr. Levinsky.
(LEVINSKY *crosses to Center to meet them hand outstretched.*)
He represents—

ARTHUR: (*Realizing who* LEVINSKY *is.*) We know what he represents.
(*He refuses to shake* LEVINSKY's *hand.*)

LEVINSKY: Good morning, Mrs. Kirk, Mr. Kirk.
(*He crosses to the Right of the Defense table and begins to go through some papers.*)

ROSE: Where's Claudia Faith?

MACMILLAN: Haggerty's bringing her up from the ward—she'll be here in a minute

ROSE: Is she all right?

MACMILLAN: Well, I, er, haven't seen her, Mrs. Kirk—perhaps—er—Mr. Levinsky—
(ROSE *looks at* LEVINSKY.)

LEVINSKY: (*Turning around.*) She's fine.

ROSE: Is she?
(*While this goes on,* HERBERT ROSENTHAL, *a psychiatrist, comes in. A mild-looking man, in a rumpled suit and glasses, he carries a clipboard with several patient files on it. He looks harried. He waves to* MACMILLAN. MACMILLAN *nods to him. He crosses Down Right and sits in first witness chair.*)

LEVINSKY: (*Crosses left of* MACMILLAN.) The food at Bellevue isn't so good, so she's lost a little weight—

ARTHUR: I told you we should have sent her some food.

LEVINSKY: But otherwise she's fine.

ROSE: Did she say anything about—

ARTHUR: Honey, she'll be here in a minute.

ROSE: I just wanted to find out if—

ARTHUR: She'll be here in a minute, honey.

HARRY: Mac.
  (*He comes back in and signals* MACMILLAN *that the judge is on his way.* MACMILLAN *leads* ROSE *and* ARTHUR *to the chairs against the wall Stage Right. They take off coats and* ARTHUR *puts them on 4th chair,* ROSE *sits in 2nd chair,* ARTHUR *in 3rd.* MACMILLAN *sits in his chair.* LEVINSKY *crosses and sits in his chair while* HARRY *takes off his uniform jacket, removes his sweater, puts it on back of his chair and puts the jacket back on. He wears a short-barrelled pistol in a belt holster. He crosses Down of witness stand. After a second, the* JUDGE *comes in; he is a small, tidy-looking man in his 60's. He wears a suit—no robe. He crosses to his chair and sits.*)
  All rise, please—his honor, the justice of the court.
  (*Everyone stands.*)
  Please be seated.
  (*They sit.*)
  Good morning, your honor.

JUDGE: Good morning, Haggerty.
  (*The* JUDGE *sits at his bench, takes a gold pencil from his inside jacket pocket and glances around the courtroom.*)

HARRY: Your honor, the criminal calendar first. This is case number four.
  (*The* JUDGE *finds the case among his papers.*)
  Your honor, for the record, I have the relatives here.
  (*He indicates for them to rise. They do so.*)

5

What is your name and address, please?
(ARTHUR *nods to* ROSE *to start.*)

ROSE: My name is Rose Kirk and I live at 30 Country Day Lane, Mount Kisco, New York. That's in Westchester. Westchester County, New York.

HARRY: What's your relation to the defendant, Mrs. Kirk?

ROSE: Mother.
(*She sits.*)

HARRY: Sir.

ARTHUR: (*Quietly.*) Arthur Kirk. Mount Kisco. Stepfather.
(*He sits.*)

RECORDER: Can I have that again?

ARTHUR: Stepfather. I married her mother.
(HARRY *exits Right doors.*)

MACMILLAN: (*Rises, crosses Up Right Center. Leaning towards* RECORDER.) Franklin Macmillan, district attorney's office, New York County. M-A-C-M-I-L-L-A-N.
(*Sits.*)

LEVINSKY: (*Stepping towards* RECORDER *Left Center.*) Aaron Levinsky, L-E-V-I-N-S-K-Y, for the defendant.
(*As he is finishing,* CLAUDIA FAITH KIRK DRAPER *comes in. She is in her early 30's, small, drawn, controlled. If she were dressed, she might be attractive, but she is not. She is wearing pajamas and a seersucker bathrobe; stenciled diagonally across the back of the robe is the word "Bellevue." On her feet are white socks and rubber thongs. She carries a thick book, two notebooks and two pencils. The first people she sees when she comes through the door are* ROSE *and* ARTHUR, *and—for a second—she breaks stride. She smiles quickly and goes to* LEVINSKY *who starts to lead her to the table.* HARRY *closes the door and stays Up Right Center.*)

CLAUDIA: Hiya, sugar: How's tricks?

(*She laughs; he frowns. Shaking his head.* CLAUDIA *turns to* JUDGE.)

Ah, a hanging judge.

(LEVINSKY *leads her to defendant's table and sits her in Up Stage chair. The* JUDGE *beckons* LEVINSKY *over and whispers to him;* LEVINSKY *goes to* CLAUDIA, *whispers to her,* HARRY *crosses Stage Left and sits in Left chair.*)

HARRY: (*Crosses Up Left Center.*) Your honor, the defendant is here. Case number four.

(*He crosses to his seat Down of middle window and sits.*)

JUDGE: Hm . . . hm . . . hm . . . This is the time set for a hearing to controvert the findings of psychiatric examinations in the matter of the People of the State of New York versus Caludia Faith Draper. Is the defendant ready, Mr.—

RECORDER: Levinsky, your honor.

LEVINSKY: (*Rises.*) The defendant is ready, your honor.

MACMILLAN: (*Rises.*) The people are ready, your honor.

(*They sit.*)

JUDGE: (*Staring at* CLAUDIA *until she turns and looks at him.*) We are not so formal here as in the other parts of the Supreme Court—we allow a good deal of leeway—but I'd like to remind everyone that this is a judicial proceeding and the rules of contempt apply. Proceed Mr. Macmillan.

MACMILLAN: (*Rises, crosses Down Right and Up Center to* JUDGE'S *bench.*) Your honor, the defendant has been indicted in the county of New York for a felony, namely manslaughter in the first degree. Because of certain facts that came to the attention of my office, People asked that the defendant be given a psychiatric evaluation to determine whether she had the capacity to stand trial on this felony indictment. This is in

7

accordance with Article seven-three-oh of the Criminal Procedure Law. The defendant was removed from the House of Detention for Women and brought to Bellevue Hospital for the evaluation. The results of that evaluation were submitted to the court, and—as you can see from the papers before you—the two examining psychiatrists found that the defendant did *not* have the capacity to stand trial. Upon being notified of the results, the defendant, in accordance with seven-three-oh-three-oh, filed a motion for a hearing to challenge. The court granted that motion and this procedure is that hearing. Your honor, only one of the examining psychiatrists is present to testify, but since their findings were the same, I'd like to have a stipulation for the absent witness.

JUDGE: Any objection?

LEVINSKY: No objection, your honor.

JUDGE: So ruled.

MACMILLAN: (*Crosses Right of Prosecutor's Table and paces Up and Down Right.*) Your honor, I'd like to call Dr. Herbert Rosenthal.
(ROSENTHAL *goes to the stand.* HARRY *takes a Bible to him.* CLAUDIA *waves and smiles as* ROSENTHAL *passes her.* LEVINSKY *touches her arm. She puts her hand down.*)

HARRY: Do you solemnly swear that the testimony you shall give in this special proceeding shall be the truth, the whole truth and nothing but the truth?

ROSENTHAL: I do.

HARRY: Be seated, please.
(ROSENTHAL *sits;* HARRY *sits.* LEVINSKY *and* CLAUDIA *takes notes throughout most of* ROSENTHAL's *testimony.*)

MACMILLAN: Dr. Rosenthal, where do you work?

ROSENTHAL: At Bellevue Hospital.

MACMILLAN: And what is your position there?

ROSENTHAL: I'm the unit chief of Ward N-O-2, the prison ward.

MACMILLAN: And how long have you—

JUDGE: Do we need all this? We know he's a psychiatrist.

LEVINSKY: (*Rises.* MACMILLAN *stops pacing.*) Your honor, since I'm a novice at these special proceedings, would it be all right if we got the qualifications on record—no offense, Dr. Rosenthal.
(The JUDGE *gestures wearily.* LEVINSKY *sits.*)

MACMILLAN: (*Continues pacing.*) And how long have you been a psychiatrist, doctor?

ROSENTHAL: Fifteen years.

MACMILLAN: Now during those fifteen years, have you conducted any examinations in connection with the capacity to stand trial in a criminal proceeding?

ROSENTHAL: Many times.

MACMILLAN: About how many examinations would you say, doctor?

ROSENTHAL: More than 200.
(LEVINSKY *and* CLAUDIA *make notes.*)

MACMILLAN: (*Stops pacing. Is Up Right Center above Prosecutor's Table.*) Dr. Rosenthal, have you examined the defendant, Claudia Draper?

ROSENTHAL: Yes, I have.

MACMILLAN: When was that, doctor?

9

ROSENTHAL: Eight days ago. Two, thirteen, seventy-nine, here at Bellevue.

MACMILLAN: What did your examination consist of?

ROSENTHAL: It consisted of questions and answers—in the usual form of a psychiatric interview—to ascertain the patient's mental condition. I determined his—I mean, her—general behavior, her attitudes, her ideation, her thought content, her various affects and the general stream of her mental condition.

MACMILLAN: Dr. Rosenthal, could you give us an idea of the substance of the examination?

ROSENTHAL: Well, when the patient came for the examination, she brought a notebook and pencil with her. I should add that I have never in 15 years of practice had a patient arrive with a notebook and pencil. She sat down, opened the notebook to a clean page, put the pencil beside the notebook and folded her hands. She did not say hello, or good morning, or volunteer any greeting. I said good morning and asked her what her notebook was for. She smiled and pointed to my notepad.

MACMILLAN: How would you describe this smile—was it a smile of hello?

ROSENTHAL: No—I'd call it a—mocking smile.
(CLAUDIA *smiles at* LEVINSKY.) Almost, er, threatening.

LEVINSKY: (*Rising.*) Your honor, I thought Mr. Macmillan asked about the substance of the examination. So far we've heard about two notebooks, a pencil and a smile. Is that the substance?

MACMILLAN: Your honor, I'm trying to give some idea of the atmosphere.

JUDGE: Is the atmosphere important?

MACMILLAN: I believe it is, your honor.

10

LEVINSKY: (*Airily, shrugging.*) Fine with me, your honor. (*He sits.*)

MACMILLAN: (*Crosses Left of Witness Stand.*) Dr. Rosenthal, when did the defendant first speak?

ROSENTHAL: She first spoke when I asked her—"Why are you here?"—that's a standard opening question.

MACMILLAN: And what did she say?

ROSENTHAL: She said, "I'm here so you can do your job." I asked her to tell me what she thought my job was—that's another standard question—and she said, "Your job is to put people away." When I asked her to explain why she believed that, she attacked me as a hypocrite and told me to "get on with my job."

CLAUDIA: (*Reading from her notebook.*) "Your job is to put people away. They don't pay you to turn me loose, do they? So why the hell don't you stop jerking me off, and get on with your job. Earn your money, Doc. Put me away."
(*The JUDGE leans in and stares at CLAUDIA, she looks at him.*)
I take better notes than him, (*To ROSENTHAL.*) don't I, doctor?

JUDGE: Mr. Levinsky, (LEVINSKY *rises.*) keep in mind our conversation.

LEVINSKY: Yes, your honor.
(*He sits and whispers to CLAUDIA.*)

MACMILLAN: Now, doctor, did you ask the defendant about the charge against her?

ROSENTHAL: I tried to ask her.

MACMILLAN: And how did she answer you?

ROSENTHAL: She told me the Constitution gave her the right not to discuss the charge with me.

MACMILLAN: (*Crosses Up Right Center.*) Did the fact that the defendant refused to discuss the charge with you—did that fact in any way influence your finding?

ROSENTHAL: Well, as part of a total context, of course, it's—

MACMILLAN: Was that fact decisive or pivotal to your finding, doctor?

ROSENTHAL: No, not decisive or pivotal.

MACMILLAN: (*Paces Up and Down Right.*) Dr. Rosenthal, in summary, could you give us a general idea of what in the defendant's behavior led to your finding that she was incapacitated?

ROSENTHAL: (MACMILLAN *stops pacing—he is Up Right.*) Well, I found her to be generally withdrawn and aloof, with a tendency towards inappropriate humor.
(CLAUDIA *laughs.*)
Suspicious, often hostile; never showing any spontaneity in answering questions. In fact, at one point I suspected a psychomotor retardation.
(CLAUDIA *reacts by slamming down her pencil.*)

MACMILLAN: What does that mean, doctor?

ROSENTHAL: Whenever I asked a question, if the patient did answer, there was a long silence between question and answer.

MACMILLAN: Every time?

ROSENTHAL: No. That's why I reserved judgment on the diagnosis of psychomotor retardation.

MACMILLAN: Dr. Rosenthal, as a result of your examination, did you come to a conclusion as to the defendant's mental condition?

ROSENTHAL: Yes. It was clear to me that the patient was severely out of touch with reality. Often, her answers to my

12

questions made no sense to me at all. She was obsessed with the idea of conspiracy and obviously regarded me as a part of one. As the examination went on, she withdrew more and more. She refused to comprehend I am a physician and here to help—at one point she accused me of trying to kill one of the other patients on the ward and—

CLAUDIA: She's six months pregnant, and he's killing her and he's killing her baby.
(*She jumps up and goes to the witness stand.* LEVINSKY *and* HARRY *also get up.*)
What's the matter, do you hate mothers?
(HARRY *grabs* CLAUDIA *by the wrists to restrain her.*)

JUDGE: Mr. Levinsky, if this proceeding is too much of a hardship for the defendant, I'll consider a request for an adjournment.

LEVINSKY: Thank you, your honor, she'll be all right.
(*He crosses to* HARRY *and touches his arm.* HARRY *lets go of* CLAUDIA. LEVINSKY *then steps in front of her and stares at her. She slowly crosses back to her chair.* LEVINSKY *follows her. She turns and looks at him, but he just stares at her until she sits.* LEVINSKY *and* HARRY *then go back to their chairs and sit.* LEVINSKY *leans in and whispers to* CLAUDIA, *then nods to the* JUDGE.)

JUDGE: Very well, go on, doctor.
(MACMILLAN *crosses in to Up Right Center.* CLAUDIA *sits staring down.*)

ROSENTHAL: She made it clear to me that she mistrusted my most innocent actions—I offered her a cup of coffee and she said, "Is the Thorazine in it? I can do without my dose of poison today."

MACMILLAN: Dr. Rosenthal, did you make a specific medical diagnosis?

ROSENTHAL: Yes. It's my professional opinion that the patient suffers from paranoid schizophrenia.
(CLAUDIA *stiffens, turning quickly and facing* ROSENTHAL.)

MACMILLAN: Based on your examination and diagnosis, do you believe that the defendant can rationally understand the charge against her?

ROSENTHAL: I don't believe so.
(CLAUDIA *turns front, shaking her head.*)

MACMILLAN: And based on this examination and diagnosis, do you believe that the defendant can consult rationally with her counsel and assist him in her defense?

ROSENTHAL: I don't believe so.

MACMILLAN: Finally, doctor, do you believe the defendant is dangerous to herself or others?

ROSENTHAL: Yes, I do.

CLAUDIA: (*Twirling her water glass.*) Look out, baby, Mama's gonna get you.
(LEVINSKY *takes her glass and puts it down. Everyone looks at* JUDGE.)

JUDGE: (*Stares at* CLAUDIA *then leans in to* DOCTOR.) Doctor, explain your danger standard, please.

ROSENTHAL: Well, your honor, I don't want to go too far out on a limb—it's not fair to science—but when a patient is paranoid, and I found this patient to be paranoid, and has this patient's history, I'd consider such a patient dangerous.

LEVINSKY: (*Rises.*) Your honor, for the record, could we have the witness define paranoid?
(*He sits.*)

ROSENTHAL: (*After a nod from the* JUDGE.) A paranoid state is a mental condition in which the patient believes that people are against him; sometimes some people, sometimes all people. Because of this belief, the patient feels continuously threatened. And when a patient feels threatened all the time, he's likely to act out his—in this case, her—violent impulses against all those supposed enemies. For example, I asked the patient if she believed I was siding with the district attorney, and she said—

CLAUDIA: Luke, eleven, twenty-three—He that is not with me is against me.
(LEVINSKY *motions to* JUDGE *he's in control.*)

ROSENTHAL: (*After a pause.*) That's what she said.

JUDGE: Does this mean she can't understand the charge?

ROSENTHAL: In this patient's case, she's so convinced that the district attorney and her parents and I are conspiring to put her away instead of letting her stand trial that I don't see how she could distinguish between a criminal charge and persecution.
(JUDGE *nods to* MACMILLAN *to continue.*)

MACMILLAN: (*Crosses Right of witness stand.*) In your professional opinion, Dr. Rosenthal, can the defendant be treated successfully?

ROSENTHAL: Good God, yes.
(*Looks at* CLAUDIA, *who waves.* LEVINSKY *touches her arm.*) She's a perfect candidate for treatment. She's intelligent, she's not insensitive and—most important—she's not too far gone.

MACMILLAN: Doctor, putting aside for a minute your role as a witness, would you like to see the defendant receive treatment before she's brought to trial?

ROSENTHAL: (MACMILLAN *crosses Up Right Center.*) Absolutely. If she had appendicitis or pneumonia, no court in the land would expect her to go to trial; they'd postpone until she recovered. We're not in the dark ages any more; we know there are diseases of the mind as well as the body. If you put this patient under the right kind of care she can be treated to the point where she can go to trial.

MACMILLAN: Dr. Rosenthal, let me ask you one more time: do you have an opinion of reasonable medical certainty that the defendant, Claudia Draper, as a result of a mental disease or defect, lacks the capacity to understand the charge against her, or the proceeding, or to assist in her own defense?

ROSENTHAL: Yes.

MACMILLAN: And what is that opinion of reasonable medical certainty?

ROSENTHAL: In my professional opinion, the patient, as a result of a mental disease or defect, does not have the capacity to understand the charge against her, or the proceeding, nor can she assist in her own defense.

MACMILLAN: Thank you, doctor. No further questions, your honor.
(*He crosses to his seat and sits.*)

JUDGE: Mr. Levinsky, do you have any questions?

LEVINSKY: (*Rising, drinks some water. Pushes in his chair and stands behind it.*) A few, your honor. Dr. Rosenthal, I'm going to go rather slowly, if you don't mind, because I'm unclear on a couple of points. Is that all right you?

ROSENTHAL: Certainly.

LEVINSKY: Thank you, I know you're a busy man. Now let's see—you're a licensed physician, aren't you?

ROSENTHAL: Of course.

16

LEVINSKY: Of course you are. I always get psychologists and psychiatrists mixed up, but psychiatrists are the ones with the M.D., right?

ROSENTAL: M.D.

LEVINSKY: (*Crosses Down of defendant's table and to Right of witness stand.*) So, you're in the practice of psychiatry, which is a branch of medicine?

ROSENTHAL: Correct.

LEVINSKY: Now, doctor, you work at Bellevue, which is a medical hospital, right?

ROSENTHAL: Yes, its a medical hospital.

LEVINSKY: Bellevue is licensed by the state of New York to provide medical and surgical diagnostic procedures and treatments, right?

ROSENTHAL: Yes.

LEVINSKY: These procedures and treatments—this practice of medicine—are to make people, sick people, well, right?

ROSENTHAL: Well, or better.

MACMILLAN: (*Rises.*) Your honor, surely counsel for the defense knows what hospitals and doctors do?

LEVINSKY: Not always, your honor. Could I have a little more rope?
(*The* JUDGE *holds up thumb and forefinger indicating about 4". MACMILLAN sits.*)
Tell me, doctor, under what conditions do the doctors at Bellevue, this medical hospital, perform these procedures and treatments?

ROSENTHAL: Underpaid conditions, ha, ha, ha.
(ROSE KIRK *also laughs.*)

Er, when a patient comes in with symptoms and he's examined, if the symptoms show the presence, or the likelihood of a condition, he's treated.

LEVINSKY: (*Crosses Left of witness stand.*) Hmmm. All right, doctor, here comes Lily Levinsky—that's my mother, your honor—she's complaining of a sore throat, the doctors examine her throat and find a growth, a tumor. What then?

ROSENTHAL: They take a section of it and send it to the lab to be tested for malignancy.

LEVINSKY: Ah, Dr. Rosenthal, you don't know my mother. She says, oh, no, you can't take a piece of my throat, it's the only throat I've got, don't touch it. What then?

ROSENTHAL: Well, they persuade her that it's in her best interest to allow the test.

LEVINSKY: Mrs. Levinsky has to sign a release, doesn't she?

ROSENTHAL: Yes, she does.

LEVINSKY: My mother says, no, she won't sign.

ROSENTHAL: They never do that.

LEVINSKY: No?

ROSENTHAL: Oh, once in a great while, in a great, great, great while, someone—a Jehovah's Witness or some crank like that—he won't sign a release.

LEVINSKY: My mother is an Orthodox Jew and sometimes a crank, and she's telling you to take your release and (*Pause.*) paper your walls with it. What then?

ROSENTHAL: The hospital would dismiss her.

LEVINSKY: Without treating her?

ROSENTHAL: Well, yes.

LEVINSKY: (*Crosses Left of* CLAUDIA.) So. One of the elements of the practice of medicine at this medical hospital is the consent of the patient?

ROSENTHAL: In many cases, yes.

LEVINSKY: Oh? Are there exceptions?

ROSENTHAL: Certainly there are exceptions. Minors are an exception, highly contagious diseases are an exception, emergencies are an exception.

LEVINSKY: (*Crosses Up of* CLAUDIA.) Is Mrs. Draper a minor?

ROSENTHAL: No, but—

LEVINSKY: (*Crosses Left of witness stand.*) Does she have smallpox, or typhoid, or diphtheria?

ROSENTHAL: No, she doesn't but—

LEVINSKY: Does she need emergency treatment?

ROSENTHAL: As a matter of fact, she does.

LEVINSKY: Isn't emergency treatment to save somebody's life?

ROSENTHAL: You're talking standards in the medical section. In the psychiatric section—

LEVINSKY: You did say psychiatry was a branch of medicine, didn't you, doctor?

ROSENTHAL: I did, and it is.

LEVINSKY: Dr. Rosenthal—

MACMILLAN: (*Rises, crosses Right of bench.*) Your honor, counsel's questions are gratuitous. The Mental Hygiene Law expressly says that—

LEVINSKY: That Dr. Rosenthal—a psychiatrist, in the practice of medicine—can examine and treat anybody any way he wants. Without that person's consent.

JUDGE: Mr. Levinsky, if you wish to challenge the provisions of the Mental Hygiene Law, this isn't the proper forum for it.

LEVINSKY: (*Crosses Center to bench.*) Of course not, your honor. All I want to do is—give some idea of the atmosphere.
(JUDGE *smiles and nods;* MACMILLAN *acknowledges* LEVINSKY'S *got him, smiles and sits.*)
Now, Dr. Rosenthal, how many defendants did you say you'd examined for their capacity to stand trial?

ROSENTHAL: More than 200.

LEVINSKY: (*Crosses to Left of defendant's table, looks at notes on pads.*) You're sure of that figure, doctor?

ROSENTHAL: Yes, more than 200.

LEVINSKY: Hmmm. And how many of these defendants did you find incapacitated?

MACMILLAN: (*Jumping up.*) Your honor, the question is irrelevant.

JUDGE: I'll allow it.
(MACMILLAN *sits.*)

ROSENTHAL: I'd have to check my records. We're talking about 15 years.

LEVINSKY: I see. Your honor, I'm not opposed to taking a short recess while we send for Dr. Rosenthal's records—
(*He sits.*)

MACMILLAN: (*Rises.*) Objection.
(MACMILLAN *sits.*)

JUDGE: Could you give us an estimate, doctor?
(LEVINSKY *rises.*)

ROSENTHAL: Oh, perhaps—80.

20

LEVINSKY: 80?

ROSENTHAL: Perhaps 90.

LEVINSKY: 90?

ROSENTHAL: Perhaps 105. Certainly no more than 105. Absolutely not. Probably less than 105.
(CLAUDIA *leans in toward* ROSENTHAL *tapping her steno pad against her hand.*)

LEVINSKY: Can we agree on 105, doctor?
(ROSENTHAL *nods.*)

RECORDER: I didn't get that.

ROSENTHAL: Yes.

LEVINSKY: (*Pushes his chair in.*) And they did go away, didn't they, doctor? They were put away?

MACMILLAN: Objection.
(*The* JUDGE *waves curtly.*)

CLAUDIA: (*Arm out to* MACMILLAN.) Overruled, Mr. Macmillan.
(JUDGE *reacts.* LEVINSKY *pushes her arm Down as he crosses Up Left of witness stand.*)

ROSENTHAL: They were hospitalized, if that's what you mean.

LEVINSKY: That's what I mean. Dr. Rosenthal, do you have a private practice?

ROSENTHAL: I wish I did, ha, ha, ha. No. I'm employed by the hospital.

LEVINSKY: So you're paid by the state?

ROSENTHAL: The city and the state.

LEVINSKY: Like Mr. Macmillan?

ROSENTHAL: It's hardly the same.

LEVINSKY: Even though you're paid by the state, you don't think of yourself as a paid agent of the state, like Mr. Macmillan?

ROSENTHAL: I certainly do not. I'm a doctor, not a prosecutor. You know, many doctors are paid by the state.

LEVINSKY: And how many of them have put 105 people away?

MACMILLAN: (*Rising.*) Your honor, the Mental Hygiene Law expressly allows—

LEVINSKY: Your honor, I know what the Mental Hygiene Law expressly allows. From the defendant's point of view, the witness is not simply "a doctor" but a paid agent of the state who has a verifiable history of putting people away—
(ROSENTHAL *begins to object.*)
I beg your pardon, doctor, you would say "committing them for prolonged treatment."

JUDGE: Mr. Levinsky, what's the purpose of this line of questioning?

LEVINSKY: Your honor, it's standard practice for counsel to question the methods and credentials of expert witnesses— particularly when the expert witness has a direct role in the case.

MACMILLAN: In a criminal proceeding, your honor.

LEVINSKY: Your honor, Article 730 is a section of the Criminal Procedure Law.

JUDGE: Proceed, Mr. Levinsky. (MACMILLAN *sits.*)

LEVINSKY: (*Taking his pad out of his pocket.*) Dr. Rosenthal, can you tell me what the defendant is charged with?

ROSENTHAL: It's a homicide charge of some sort—manslaughter, first-degree manslaughter.

LEVINSKY: Do you know the elements of first-degree manslaughter?

ROSENTHAL: No, I'm not a lawyer.

LEVINSKY: (*Smiles at* ROSENTHAL *then crosses down to Down Left.*) When you asked the defendant about the charge, did you happen to ask about the circumstances of the alleged crime?

ROSENTHAL: Yes, of course.

LEVINSKY: (*Left of his chair.*) Did you happen to ask about the circumstances more than once?

ROSENTHAL: (*Opening his notepad.*) —Well—

LEVINSKY: What's the matter, doctor, do you have a psychomotor retardation?

MACMILLAN: (*Rises.*) Your honor?
(*The* JUDGE *hides a smile and waggles a finger at* LEVINSKY. LEVINSKY *yields.* MACMILLAN *sits.*)

ROSENTHAL: Yes, I did.

LEVINSKY: About how many times did you ask her?

ROSENTHAL: Three.

LEVINSKY: (*Leaning on back of his chair.*) Three times. Hadn't the defendant told you that that was between her and her lawyer?

ROSENTHAL: You must comprehend that my questions were purely from a psychiatric perspective—a medical, psychiatric perspective. I wasn't trying to manipulate her into incriminating herself.

LEVINSKY: (*Crosses Left of witness stand.*) Of course. A medical perspective. You're a doctor and you always refer to the

23

defendant as the patient. The doctor–patient relationship is a privileged one, isn't it?

ROSENTHAL: Yes.

LEVINSKY: Except that your conversation with the defendant was not privileged, was it, doctor?

MACMILLAN: (*Rises.* LEVINSKY *slowly crosses Center.*) Your honor, I know Mr. Levinsky is unacquainted with Article 730, so I'd like to assure him that all discussion of a criminal act between a defendant and an examining psychiatrist is inadmissible.

LEVINSKY: Thank you, Mr. Macmillan.

MACMILLAN: You're welcome, Mr. Levinsky.
(*Sits.*)

LEVINSKY: (*Crosses Right of witness stand.*) But there's nothing to stop you from taking what you hear to the district attorney, is there, doctor?

ROSENTHAL: (*Reading from an index card taped to clipboard. Taps it with pencil.*) "Technically, this interview isn't confidential and privileged,
(LEVINSKY *crosses Left of defendant table.* ROSENTHAL *pauses then continues.*)
but I'm here to help you, and you can trust me not to repeat any damaging or incriminating material." I read that to all my patients, and I read it to this one. She called me a lair.

CLAUDIA: Liar.

LEVINSKY: (*After a glance at* CLAUDIA.) Doctor, you described the defendant as—withdrawn, aloof, suspicious, often hostile and—

CLAUDIA: With a tendency to inappropriate humor.

24

LEVINSKY: (*Quickly before the* JUDGE *can intervene. To* CLAU-
DIA.) Thank you.
(*Crosses Left of witness stand.*)
Doctor, do you think if you'd examined her under different
circumstances, she might have behaved differently?

ROSENTHAL: It's not likely.

LEVINSKY: So you believe the circumstances of your examination—the defendant a prisoner, you a paid agent of the state—

MACMILLAN: (*Rises.*) Objection!
(JUDGE *holds up his hand.* MACMILLAN *sits.*)

LEVINSKY: —the absence of confidentiality—all these conditions had no effect—no effect—on the way the defendant
responded?

ROSENTHAL: Your point is valid—if we were talking about a
normal person. Obviously, normal people behave differently
in different contexts. This patient is not normal. She has been
diagnosed as a paranoid schizophrenic.

LEVINSKY: Of course. So her behavior ignores the conditions,
right?

ROSENTHAL: Not ignores. Distorts.

LEVINSKY: You mean, say, like her attitude towards Thorazine?

ROSENTHAL: Yes, a very good example. "I can do without my
dose of poison today." It's precisely that sort of thing that
demonstrates how out of touch with reality she is. Thorazine
is not poison; it's medicine.

LEVINSKY: Of course. A medicine. Did the defendant complain
of any reactions to this medicine? You have your notes,
doctor.

ROSENTHAL: (*Opens notepad.*) There seems to be an item to
that effect.

LEVINSKY: What does it say?

ROSENTHAL: "Patient complains of sore throat, dry mouth, nasal congestion and fever."

LEVINSKY: So, naturally, doctor, you gave her some medical tests?

ROSENTHAL: (*Continues looking through notes.*) Er, I don't see a record of that.

LEVINSKY: No urine test.

ROSENTHAL: No.

LEVINSKY: No differential smear.

ROSENTHAL: No.

LEVINSKY: No white blood count?

ROSENTHAL: I don't see a record of that.

LEVINSKY: But you would say that in resisting the Thorazine the defendant was distorting the conditions and ignoring reality?

ROSENTHAL: Yes, I would. She needed the Thorazine to moderate her agitation, and it is not poison.

LEVINSKY: (*Crosses Down around defendant's table to behind his chair.*) Of course. It's an innocent medicine that gave her a sore throat, dry mouth, nasal congestion and fever. But it's not poison.

ROSENTHAL: To believe medicine is poison is deluded, paranoid.

LEVINSKY: Ah, yes, paranoid. Which makes her dangerous to herself and others, right?

ROSENTHAL: In my professional opinion.

LEVINSKY: (*Crosses Left of* CLAUDIA, *puts his hands on her shoulder.*) Tell me, doctor, did you ever see the defendant try to injure herself?

ROSENTHAL: No, not personally.

LEVINSKY: Did you ever see her try to injure anybody else?

ROSENTHAL: No, not personally.

LEVINSKY: (*Crosses Left of witness stand.*) Did you ever hear her threaten to hurt herself?

ROSENTHAL: No.

LEVINSKY: Did you ever hear her threaten to hurt anybody else?

ROSENTHAL: No.

LEVINSKY: Did somebody else at Bellevue ever see her hurt herself or anybody else, or threaten to hurt herself or anybody else?

ROSENTHAL: (*Looking at his file.*) Well, let me see—

LEVINSKY: Take your time, doctor.

ROSENTHAL: No, I don't see a notation to that effect. Of course, it might not have been reported.

LEVINSKY: But as far as you know, the defendant has never threatened or harmed anyone, right?

ROSENTHAL: She did kill a man.
(CLAUDIA *throws her pencil down.*)

LEVINSKY: (*Angry. Crosses Center-Right of witness stand.*) Your honor, I know the witness is a doctor and not a laywer, but could the court explain to him that as far as the law is concerned the defendant is innocent?

JUDGE: I think you've explained it well enough, Mr. Levinsky.
(*To* RECORDER.)
Strike "She did kill a man."

LEVINSKY: So far as you know the defendant has never threatened or harmed anyone?

ROSENTHAL: So far as I know.

LEVINSKY: Well, doctor, who is the defendant dangerous to?

ROSENTHAL: (*Pause.*) Perhaps her parents.

LEVINSKY: (*Looking at them.*) Anyone else?

ROSENTHAL: Perhaps the district attorney.

LEVINSKY: Mr. Macmillan?
(*Staring at him, doubtfully.*)
Hmmm. Anyone else?

ROSENTHAL: Well—I can't think of anyone else right at this moment.

LEVINSKY: What about you, doctor? Do you think the defendant is dangerous to you?
(CLAUDIA *leans forward towards* ROSENTHAL *smiling and begins to slide herself and chair towards* ROSENTHAL. HARRY *puts his hand on back of chair.*)

ROSENTHAL: (*Glancing at* CLAUDIA, *who smiles.*) Well—perhaps. Under certain circumstances, perhaps.

LEVINSKY: Would you feel safer if the defendant were hospitalized?

ROSENTHAL: I suppose if I thought about it I might feel safer.
(CLAUDIA *angrily writes some notes.*)

LEVINSKY: (*Crosses Left of his chair.*) So to some degree you have more than a simple professional interest in the outcome of this proceeding?

ROSENTHAL: (*As it sinks in.*) I have absolutely no personal interest in the outcome of this proceeding, I want to see this patient hospitalized solely for her own good, and I find your implication insulting and revolting.

LEVINSKY: (*Crosses Left of* CLAUDIA.) My apologies, doctor. Now, as I grasp it, you diagnosed the defendant as suffering from a mental disease, right?

ROSENTHAL: Yes, I did.

LEVINSKY: (*Crosses Left of his chair.*) Has the defendant ever been treated or hospitalized for this mental disease?

ROSENTHAL: Not to my knowledge, no.

LEVINSKY: So the only evidence that she's mentally ill is your say-so?

ROSENTHAL: And Dr. Alvarez's.

LEVINSKY: So you're asking the court to commit the defendant purely on your say-so?

ROSENTHAL: That's a gross simplifica—

LEVINSKY: Aren't you asking the court to commit her?

ROSENTHAL: Yes, but—

LEVINSKY: (*Crosses Down of defendant's table and Up Center, Right of witness stand.*) On the basis of one 50-minute examination conducted in a prison ward against the defendant's will, right?

ROSENTHAL: You're leaving out—

LEVINSKY: Dr. Rosenthal, are you not the person who has labeled the defendant a paranoid schizophrenic and recommended that she be committed?

ROSENTHAL: Yes, but—

LEVINSKY: But, what?

ROSENTHAL: You're making it sound so arbitrary. I don't do this lightly.

29

LEVINSKY: What have I left out, doctor?

ROSENTHAL: The behavior that led to my diagnosis.

LEVINSKY: (*Crosses quickly Left of his chair.* CLAUDIA *writes.*) Of course, the behavior. She was belligerent?

ROSENTHAL: Not exactly.

LEVINSKY: Defiant?

ROSENTHAL: Part of the time.

LEVINSKY: (*Writes on pad.*) Okay, defiant.

ROSENTHAL: No, no. I don't like that label. Let's be precise here. The point is her behavior was completely out of keeping with the context. The proper term would be negativistic. (LEVINSKY *and* CLAUDIA *write this down.*)

LEVINSKY: What does that mean?

ROSENTHAL: A reaction opposed to the normal reaction expected in a given situation.

LEVINSKY: (*Slowly and carefully crosses Left of witness stand.*) A reaction opposed to the normal reaction expected in a given situation.

ROSENTHAL: Yes.

LEVINSKY: Expected by whom?

ROSENTHAL: By the— (*He stops abruptly.*)

LEVINSKY: Expected by whom?

ROSENTHAL: By the psychiatrist doing the examination.

LEVINSKY: (*Crosses Left of* CLAUDIA.) Thank you, doctor, I have no more questions.

ROSENTHAL: Just a minute, just a minute.

LEVINSKY: (*Crosses Left of his chair.*) I have no more questions, your honor.

ROSENTHAL: (*To the* JUDGE.) May I say something?

JUDGE: It was neatly done, Mr. Levinsky,
(CLAUDIA *slaps* LEVINSKY'*s arm, pleased. He sits.*)
but this isn't the Criminal Courts. Go ahead, doctor.
(CLAUDIA *reacts.* LEVINSKY *calms her.*)

ROSENTHAL: (*Puts notepad on floor Right of chair and leans forward on railing.*) All I want to say is this. This is a sick person, whom we're trying to help. What you are doing with your legal tricks is depriving this girl of treatment, and you had better understand that. Now, I want her to get better, and the only place she's going to get better is in a hospital. I believe that and so does the district attorney. Now, she doesn't believe that, but no patient ever does. Any doctor will tell you, especially any doctor in psychiatry, that the patient almost never knows what's good for him. There is a wider context here than the law. This girl has a history and you're ignoring it. A broken home, a broken marriage, disillusion, despair, terror, homicidal rage—we are not talking about a "defendant," we are talking about a very troubled patient. We're not talking about a girl from the streets—we're talking about a nice, bright middle-class girl who couldn't cope and broke down. When a girl like this one becomes a prostitute and kills one of her customers, (LEVINSKY *jumps up.* CLAUDIA *faces* ROSENTHAL. JUDGE *holds his hand up stopping* LEVINSKY *who then leans against Left railing.*)
we're talking about breakdown. Breakdown. When there's breakdown, it's our job to put the pieces back together. I want to tell you that's not done in a courtroom or a prison, that's done in a hospital.
(ROSENTHAL *collects notepad and begins to leave stand.* ROSENTHAL *and* ARTHUR *nod approvingly to each other.*)

LEVINSKY: (*Trying to contain his rage and stopping* ROSENTHAL.) Did you make love to the defendant?

ROSENTHAL: (*Sitting.*) What?

LEVINSKY: Did you make love to the defendant?

ROSENTHAL: Of course not.

LEVINSKY: (*Crosses Down of table to Left of witness stand.*) Did she proposition you?

ROSENTHAL: No.

LEVINSKY: Did she touch you?

ROSENTHAL: No.

LEVINSKY: Did she take off her clothes?

ROSENTHAL: No.

LEVINSKY: Did she ask you for money?

ROSENTHAL: No.

LEVINSKY: Did she tell you she'd been a prostitute?

ROSENTHAL: No.

LEVINSKY: Did you ask her if she'd been a prostitute?

ROSENTHAL: Yes.

LEVINSKY: And what did she answer? Doctor, what did she answer?

ROSENTHAL: She said, "Whoring is getting paid for work you don't want to do."

LEVINSKY: Has the defendant been charged with prostitution?

ROSENTHAL: I don't know.

LEVINSKY: Maybe Mr. Macmillan knows. Mr. Macmillan.

(MACMILLAN *is slowly looking at his papers.*)
Mr. Macmillan!!!

MACMILLAN: There's no charge of prostitution.

LEVINSKY: So you have no knowledge—no personal, no professional knowledge—that the defendant was ever a prostitute,
right?

ROSENTHAL: Yes, that's right.

LEVINSKY: (*Crosses Center Right of witness stand.*) And other
than what the district attorney has told you, you have no
knowledge—no personal, no professional knowledge—that
the defendant ever killed anyone, right?

ROSENTHAL: Well—

LEVINSKY: (*Yelling.*) Right?

ROSENTHAL: Yes, that right.

CLAUDIA: (*Rises.*) Right!
(MACMILLAN *and* HARRY *rise.*)

LEVINSKY: (*Quickly, hands up.*) I have no more questions.
(*He crosses to* CLAUDIA, *makes her sit, then he sits.*)

MACMILLAN: With your permission, your honor, I'd like to
save my redirect for later.
(*He sits. The* JUDGE *nods.*)

HARRY: You can step down, doctor.
(ROSENTHAL *goes to his seat.* HARRY *sits.*)

MACMILLAN: (*Rises.*) Your honor, I'd like to call the defendant's mother, Mrs. Kirk.
(CLAUDIA, *surprised, grabs* LEVINSKY. ROSE *stands.*)

LEVINSKY: (*Rising.*) Your honor, can the smokers have a short
recess?

(MACMILLAN *starts toward bench to object.*)

JUDGE: (*Glances at* CLAUDIA.) We'll take a few minutes.
(JUDGE *rises, exits Up Stage door,* RECORDER *exits Right door and* MACMILLAN *looks at* LEVINSKY *who shrugs.* MACMILLAN *throws his pad on table and exits Right door.* LEVINSKY *sits.* ROSE *and* ARTHUR *hesitate.* ROSE *then sits.* HARRY *rises. Stands Up of his chair.* ROSENTHAL *remains seated writing on his notepad.*)

LEVINSKY: Listen, if you don't keep your mouth shut, he's going to send you right back. Get it through your head that it's their game and their rules, and the rules aren't going to change because you don't like them. You've made it hard enough for me as it is; don't make it harder.

CLAUDIA: Poor baby.

LEVINSKY: I don't want to lose this because you won't play the game. You'll play, and you'll play our way, or you'll be wearing that bathrobe till you're collecting Social Security. Do you hear me? I said, do you hear me?

CLAUDIA: I'm going to have a cigarette.

LEVINSKY: (*Rises.*) Harry, do me a favor and have a cigarette with Mrs. Draper. I have to make a couple of calls.
(LEVINSKY *takes his briefcase and exits Stage Right door.* CLAUDIA *rises crosses Right of* HARRY, ROSE *and* ARTHUR *rise.*)

CLAUDIA: Do you have any matches, Harry?

HARRY: Yeah—
(HARRY *indicates for them to leave courtroom.* CLAUDIA *with cigarette in mouth, takes her notepad from the table and begins to leave. As she does,* ROSE *makes up her mind and goes toward* CLAUDIA, ARTHUR *following.* CLAUDIA *seeing* ROSE *come forward stops Left Center.* ROSE *is Center with*

34

ARTHUR *to her Right, she stops for a moment then takes a step towards* CLAUDIA, CLAUDIA *takes a step back.* HARRY *is Right of* CLAUDIA'*s chair. There is a space of about five feet as mother and daughter face each other.*)

ROSE: Hello, darling.

(CLAUDIA *says nothing.*)

Er, how are you? You look thin. Your father wanted to send you a pie but—a lamb and carrot pie—we brought you some cigarettes but they wouldn't let us give them to you.

(ARTHUR *runs back to his chair, takes a carton of cigarettes out of his coat pocket and returns Right of* ROSE.)

Your father lost his temper but they still wouldn't let us give— A whole carton—

ARTHUR: (*Holding out the carton to* CLAUDIA.) Low tar. See? The lowest tar and nicotine of any cigarette on the market. There's a filter on top of the filter, so it blocks all the tar and nicotine. You don't get cancer with these. Of course, you don't taste anything,

(CLAUDIA *turns and looks front.*)

but what the hell? Don't they feed you anything? You look like a ghost.

ROSE: Mr. Levinsky said the food wasn't too good. Is that true, darling? I like him. He seems very bright. Is he bright?

(CLAUDIA *turns and stares at* ROSE.)

You look tired. Am I making you tired? Just say so if I am. I don't want to make you tired. If you don't want to talk, it's all right. We can talk later. Art, we can talk to her later.

HARRY: Mrs. Draper, I'm not meant to leave you alone, but if you want to talk to—

CLAUDIA: (*Taking the cigarette out of her mouth.*) No.

(CLAUDIA *motions to* HARRY *that she wants to leave. He gestures "after you." She crosses down of* ROSE *and* ARTHUR *and heads for the door.* HARRY *follows her.*)

ROSE: Claudia, we'll talk later. We love you.
(CLAUDIA *stops at the door, turns around and takes a few steps Down Stage.* HARRY *is to her right.*)

CLAUDIA: What?

ARTHUR: We love you.

ROSE: Do you know that, darling? We love you.

CLAUDIA: We love you.

ROSE: Yes.

CLAUDIA: We love you.
(ROSE *and* ARTHUR *look at each other puzzled.*)
One more time. We— Come on, we—
(*Again, they glance at each other.*)

ROSE and ARTHUR: We—

CLAUDIA: Love—

ROSE and ARTHUR: Love—

CLAUDIA: You.

ROSE and ARTHUR: You.

CLAUDIA: Thank you.
(*She smiles, salutes and walks out.* HARRY *follows her.* ROSE *looks slapped.* ARTHUR *hands the carton of cigarettes to* ROSE, *who looks at it and forces it back on him.* ROSE *pushes cigarettes away.*)

Blackout

Act Two

*A few minutes later. As the lights come up, everyone is back
except the* JUDGE *and the* RECORDER. CLAUDIA *is in her seat, her
notebook in front of her.* LEVINSKY *is sitting in his chair,
writing something on his pad.* MACMILLAN *is at his table talking
to* ROSE *and* ARTHUR *who are sitting rigidly in their chairs,*
ROSENTHAL *in his chair,* HARRY *stands Down Stage of the
witness stand. The* RECORDER *enters, closing the door, and
takes her seat. The* JUDGE *enters and goes toward the bench.*

HARRY: Remain seated, please.

JUDGE: (*After sitting.*) Proceed, Mr. Macmillan.

MACMILLAN: (*Rising.*) I'd like to call Mrs. Kirk, your honor.
(ROSE *stands and crosses to witness stand.* HARRY *gets the
Bible and holds it before her. She places her left hand on it
and raises her right hand.*)

HARRY: Do you solemnly swear that the testimony you shall
give in this special proceeding shall be the truth, the whole
truth and nothing but the truth?

ROSE: (*Nearly inaudible.*) I do.
(HARRY *sits.*)

JUDGE: Speak up, please, Mrs. Kirk.

37

ROSE: I'm sorry, sir. I do. Your honor. (*She sits.*)

JUDGE: Mrs. Kirk, have you ever testified in a courtroom before?

ROSE: No, sir. No, your honor.

JUDGE: Just speak clearly and answer the questions in your own words. We're here to listen to you. Proceed, Mr. Macmillan.

MACMILLAN: (*Crosses Left of witness stand.*) Mrs. Kirk, the defendant, Mrs. Draper, is your daughter, is that correct?

ROSE: Yes.

MACMILLAN: Do you have any other children, Mrs. Kirk?

ROSE: No, no we don't.

MACMILLAN: You and your daughter's father were divorced, were you not?

ROSE: Yes.

MACMILLAN: Was it an acrimonious divorce, Mrs. Kirk?

ROSE: Oh, no, not at all. We're civilized people. My husband— I'm talking about Claudia Faith's father—came back from the military—he served in Korea and won a Silver Star—he came back, and a little bit after that, six months, five months, we were divorced.

MACMILLAN: And how old was your daughter, Mrs. Kirk?

ROSE: Five. Five years old. I just want to assure you it wasn't acrimonious. As I recall, we even wished each other luck; it was that easy.
(CLAUDIA *writes a note and shows it to* LEVINSKY. ROSE *sees this. As she again speaks* MACMILLAN *crosses Up Left Center to block her view of* CLAUDIA.)
Now, understand, we might have exchanged a few harsh words. When he first walked into the bedroom and told me he

was leaving, I recall we exchanged a few cross words, but other than that one time—when he walked into the bedroom with his suitcase—it was friendly.

MACMILLAN: (*Crosses back to Left of witness stand.*) And your daughter did not react badly to it?

ROSE: She was just fine. After all, she was only five. Sure, she asked about him once in a while but it was, you know, the way children do—is daddy fighting another war—that kind of thing.

MACMILLAN: And how soon after your divorce did you marry Mr. Kirk?

ROSE: Eleven months. Nearly a year.

MACMILLAN: And how did your daughter get along with Mr. Kirk?

ROSE: Oh, fine. It was love at first sight for both of them. (CLAUDIA *glances at* ARTHUR.)

MACMILLAN: (*Crosses Up Right Center above prosecutor's table.*) Mrs. Kirk, can you tell us when you first noticed any changes in her behavior?

ROSE: By the time she was in the 6th grade—she was around eleven.

MACMILLAN: Can you describe those changes for us?

ROSE: She started to keep to herself, and not like an ordinary girl, either. I was a young girl; I know there's an age when you need to have a few secrets from grownups; no young girl wants her parents to know everything, it's not normal. We didn't worry about it at first because she kept changing—one day she wouldn't talk to me at all and treat Art—Mr. Kirk—as if he had the plague—and the next, she'd be all cuddly, mama, this, and daddy that, but then it got worse—she acted as if she didn't trust us at all.

MACMILLAN: She withdrew from you?

ROSE: By the time she was in high school, she'd sneak out before we got up, and either come home just before bedtime, or not come home at all—

MACMILLAN: Did you or your husband talk to her about her behavior?

ROSE: We tried, we didn't get very far.

MACMILLAN: Did you or your husband try taking her to someone—a guidance counsellor say—for advice or help?

ROSE: You have to understand that Mr. Kirk believed it was only a matter of discipline. He said she needed a good strong talking-to. And I agreed with him. We don't believe in washing our dirty linen in public. In my family, we help our own.

MACMILLAN: Mrs. Kirk, do you have any idea what caused her behavior?

ROSE: No; she's my only child and I wanted her. She was wanted—I wasn't married at the end of a shotgun. When she was born, I was so happy I went around singing. I remember sitting in the kitchen and nursing her and whispering to her that things would be different for her. I promised her that her home would be filled with love, and I kept my word. I kept my word when I was with Bill and once I married Art I kept my word even more. I don't understand it, not to this day. For a time, I thought it was my husband—Bill, I mean; the agreement gave him custody on weekends and I guessed he was telling her terrible things about me and Art. Then, I thought—God, I thought of everything. One night I stayed up and made a list: I wrote down everything I'd done and how I could have done it differently.

(*She looks at* CLAUDIA.)

Was I too stern, was I too fussy,
(CLAUDIA *turns and faces* ROSE,)
was I too protective, was I too pushy? Did I punish her for
the wrong things? Did I pick and choose her friends? Did I
ignore her when she was unhappy? Did I humiliate her in
front of strangers?
(CLAUDIA *looks away.*)
Did I set a bad example?
(ROSE *looks at* MACMILLAN *again.*)
Every mother makes those mistakes, and I'm sure I made
them sometimes. But not enough times for her to carry on the
way she did. Not enough times for her to drink and lie and
cut school and not talk to me and not kiss me and not touch
me. Not enough times for that.

MACMILLAN: (*Cross to Right of witness stand.*) And you say
this behavior didn't stop?

ROSE: Not while she was at home. We didn't see much of her
once she went away to college, and after she met Peter we
never saw her alone. They always visited together.

MACMILLAN: Peter Draper, the man she married?
(*He crosses to Up Right Center.*)

ROSE: He was in law school and she was a junior. No, a
sophomore.

MACMILLAN: (*Referring to notes.*) And they were married in
1968?

ROSE: June 15, 1968. It was an Episcopal ceremony.

MACMILLAN: (*Crosses Left of witness stand.*) And her marriage
collapsed, didn't it?

ROSE: Yes, it did. I found out from a friend. An acquaintance,
really.

MACMILLAN: Your daughter did not tell you?

ROSE: I called her and said, is it true? And she said, it's true. And there was a big silence. So I said, come home, stay with us till you feel better. No, thank you, I'm staying in the city. Now I swear to you I could hear the tears in her voice. Staying in the city is stupid. Stupid. A woman after a divorce—that's a terrible time. She's by herself, she doesn't know what's going on, she can make mistakes in the city if there's nobody there to help. Little mistakes. Oh, it's easy enough to shop for groceries and wash clothes, but there are other things. She has to deal with new people, find a job, open bank accounts, see if there's a way to put her life in order. A city is a lonely place for a divorced woman. I know I belong to an earlier generation, but men have funny ideas about divorced women. They think, well, I don't have to tell you what they think. A divorced woman is a target. She hasn't had much practice handling men. She can think she's doing fine but she can fall prey to any polite man who comes along, any man with a suit that fits and shoes

(CLAUDIA *looks at* ARTHUR.)

that are shined and a few dollars in his pocket. It's easy to fall prey. There she is, alone in her room still young, still pretty, perhaps with a child to care for, her husband gone, who knows where, who knows with whom, gone without a kind word, without a hug, gone. Gone.

(ROSE *has vanished inside.* CLAUDIA *is watching her intently.* ROSE *comes out.*)

She should have come home.

MACMILLAN: (*Crosses Up Right Center.*) And did you keep in touch with her, Mrs. Kirk?

ROSE: I called and she—she said, hello and then goodbye. Hello-goodbye. Like that. Nothing in between. Hello-goodbye, hello-goodbye. It was almost funny, she sounded like one of those tapes, hello-goodbye. So instead of calling I wrote and—and I wrote and—

(*She pulls a batch of letters from her purse.*)
I wanted to stay in touch, so I wrote, and these are the letters.
Right here. I thought I should bring them. I thought you
should see them because they're marked, you see? All of
them, every single one, in exactly the same way. Now that's
odd; you must agree that's odd, so I felt I should bring them
to show you how odd that is. The same mark on every—
(*To* CLAUDIA.)
Is this your handwriting?
(*She raises her voice.* CLAUDIA *reels around and faces her.*)
Answer me, is this your handwriting? Is this your "addressee
unknown"? Addressee unknown. Addressee unknown? There
are thirty-one letters in my hand, and they are all,
(*Rises.*)
every single one is—addressee unknown.
(*She hurls the letters to the floor in front of* CLAUDIA, *who
reaches for them.* LEVINSKY *stops her;* MACMILLAN *crosses
to* Right *of witness stand, comforts* ROSE *who sits.* HARRY
picks them up, gives them to MACMILLAN, *who gives them to*
ARTHUR *who had crossed Up Right Center.* ROSENTHAL *stands
in front of his chair.* MACMILLAN *crosses with* ARTHUR *Right.*
ARTHUR, ROSENTHAL, LEVINSKY *and* HARRY *sit.*)

JUDGE: Would you like to take a short break, Mrs. Kirk?

ROSE: (*Composing herself.*) I'm fine. I'm fine.

JUDGE: I realize that this is a strain for you and if you want
a recess, please ask for it.

ROSE: I am fine.
(*The* JUDGE *nods to* MACMILLAN.)

MACMILLAN: (*Crosses Up Right Center.*) Mrs. Kirk, when did
you last hear from your daughter?

ROSE: When I called her: Hello-goodbye.

MACMILLAN: And when she was arrested?

ROSE: She didn't call. Peter called, and said she was in jail.

MACMILLAN: And you immediately went to visit her?

ROSE: She wouldn't see us.

MACMILLAN: And did you hire an attorney for her?

ROSE: The best Mr. Kirk could find—Stanley Middleton.

MACMILLAN: And your daughter fired him, didn't she?

ROSE: Yes.

MACMILLAN: In other words, your daughter has continuously and progressively withdrawn from you for nearly 20 years, and since the breakup of her marriage has refused to have anything to do with you—you have had no contact?

ROSE: Not till today. If you can call that contact.

MACMILLAN: (*Crosses Down right.*) Now, Mrs. Kirk, I know you're not a doctor, but—

LEVINSKY: (*Rises.*) Your honor, surely Mr. Macmillan is not going to ask the witness for a medical opinion—

MACMILLAN: I simply want to ask whether as a parent—solely as a parent—
(JUDGE *motions* LEVINSKY *to sit. He does.*)
you'd like to see your daughter receive treatment.
(MACMILLAN *crosses Left of witness stand.*)
Before you answer, put out of your head any question of a crime or a trial. Do you want to see your daughter, Claudia Faith, receive treatment?

ROSE: (*After a pause.*) It's a very hard thing to swallow, that your own flesh and blood is—we've never had any trouble in my family and I'm not used to the idea of—
(*She looks at* CLAUDIA.)
I'm sorry, darling.

44

(*To* MACMILLAN.)
Yes.

MACMILLAN: If she were not in custody and you had the opportunity to pay for treatment, would you?

ROSE: (*After a glance at* ARTHUR.) Yes, we would.

MACMILLAN: (*Crosses Up Right Center.*)
Mrs. Kirk, I have one last question. Do you—

ROSE: (*Cutting in—To* JUDGE.) Your honor, I know it's a terrible thing to hear a mother say her daughter is—is—but I can't hide from the truth. It's not her fault. When they told me what she did, when they told me about the—the men, I knew it wasn't her fault. She's my own daughter, she couldn't do that and be in her right mind. She only loved one man in her life. I know how much she loved him. Her husband. Your honor, they were married in a church, an Episcopal church; the minister had green eyes, you never see an Episcopal minister with green eyes. I dressed her myself. She wore white; it was a June wedding and she wore white. I brushed her hair, I painted her nails—clear, colorless nail polish, clear as her heart, clear as her eyes. A bride must have clear eyes on her wedding day, otherwise it's bad luck.
(*Pointing to* ARTHUR.)
He held her arm, he led her down the aisle; Bill wanted to give her away but I wouldn't permit it; it was Art's right. He danced with her, I think he danced with her more than Peter did.
(CLAUDIA *looks at her.*)
Waltzes and fox trots and sambas and rhumbas, even a tango. Darling, don't you remember how your father danced with you? How he danced with you till you got dizzy?

CLAUDIA: My father didn't dance with me. You wouldn't let him.

45

ROSE: He lied to me. He lied and lied and lied and lied. Rose, he said, I love you, I love you more than life itself, I'll never look at another woman, there are no other women, can't you feel it when I touch you, Rose, there'll never be anyone else. Oh he lied. Do you know how many there were? Do you have any idea? He was like a stray cat; he couldn't pass a skirt without lifting it. He never loved me, darling. Never. He walked out through the door, with his one suitcase, that's what he took to her, his one suitcase, he walked out through the door and left me with you. He never loved me.

CLAUDIA: He loved you, Mama.

ROSE: He left me with you and six dollars and thirty-one cents. That's how much he loved me: six dollars and thirty-one cents worth.

CLAUDIA: He loved you, Mama.
(Turns front.)

MACMILLAN: *(Crosses Center Right of witness stand.)* Mrs. Kirk, do you love your daughter?
(Crying ROSE *nods, yes.)*

RECORDER: Can she say it, for the record?

ROSE: *(Recovering.)* I love my daughter.

MACMILLAN: *(Crosses Right and sits.)* Thank you, Mrs. Kirk. I have no further questions, your honor.

JUDGE: Mr. Levinsky?
*(*LEVINSKY *gets up slowly;* CLAUDIA *grabs his arm and whispers to him. He says something to her.* ROSE *wipes her eyes and nose with a hanky.)*

LEVINSKY: *(Behind his chair.)* Mrs. Kirk, would you like to take a minute?
*(*ROSE *shakes her head, no. He crosses Right of witness stand.)*

You told Mr. Macmillan that you and the defendant's father—
(CLAUDIA *taps the table with her glass.*)
Could we strike that, your honor?

JUDGE: Strike it.

LEVINSKY: You testified that when the defendant was in high school—
(CLAUDIA *taps again.* LEVINSKY *turns to look at her. She shakes her head. He shrugs.*)
Your honor, I have no questions.
(LEVINSKY *crosses to his chair and sits.*)

HARRY: (*Rises.*) You can step down, Mrs. Kirk.
(ROSE *goes back to her seat;* ARTHUR *gets up.* LEVINSKY *whispers something to* CLAUDIA *and she pulls away from him.* MACMILLAN *turns to tell* ARTHUR *he's next.*)

MACMILLAN: (*Rises.*) Your honor, I'd like to call the defendant's stepfather, Arthur Kirk.
(ARTHUR *pats* ROSE, *gives her the envelopes and goes to the stand.* HARRY *comes with the Bible.* ARTHUR *puts wrong hand on Bible,* HARRY *corrects him.* MACMILLAN *paces Up and Down Right.*)

HARRY: Do you solemnly swear that the testimony you shall give in this special proceeding shall be the truth, the whole truth and nothing but the truth?

ARTHUR: (*Loudly and confidently.*) I do.

HARRY: Be seated, please.
(HARRY *and* ARTHUR *sit.*)

MACMILLAN: (*Pacing.*) Mr. Kirk, how long have you and Mrs. Kirk been married?

ARTHUR: It'll be 24 years next month. On the eleventh.

MACMILLAN: (*Crosses Up Right Center.*) And you've known the defendant all that time?

ARTHUR: I've known her nearly 25 years. I met her when I was courting her mother. I taught her how to make spitballs.

MACMILLAN: Like your wife, did you notice these changes in her behavior?

ARTHUR: I was there and I saw it all.

MACMILLAN: Now Mrs. Kirk told us that your daughter—

ARTHUR: Stepdaughter. Got to keep the record straight.

MACMILLAN: Your stepdaughter was avoiding you—

ARTHUR: She was avoiding both of us.

MACMILLAN: Why do you think she was behaving so oddly?

ARTHUR: I'll tell you. I don't agree with Mrs. Kirk. It was Bill, all right. Now I know he won medals, and he pulled eight men out of a burning tank, and he was a real big hero, but that doesn't give him the right to run around on a woman and leave her flat with a kid.

MACMILLAN: Mr. Kirk, if you would just—

ARTHUR: Let me finish, would ya. I know how the world works, but if you're going to cheat, you don't rub your wife's nose in it. I know there are people in this world, you can offer them prime steak every night, they still want lamb or chicken. Fine. It's a big world and there's room in it for all kinds of tastes. But you don't need to walk out. You want your little something on the side, you keep it quiet, you behave, you're a husband and a father. A husband, a father, that's responsibility. There's nothing in the Constitution that says every marriage has got to be happy. I know 50 couples and I'll bet not one of them is happy. A marriage is a deal, here's the

piece of paper, you do this, I'll do that, and the deal works. It's not so complicated if you believe in deals. I've never seen a marriage certificate yet had the word "happy" in it. As far as I'm concerned, a man can chase sheep, just so long as he comes home and takes care of his family. Bill didn't. (*Points at* ROSE.)
Bill took a walk.

MACMILLAN: And how did that contrib—

ARTHUR: First he walked, then he came back and filled her head with all kinds of stories. I don't know what he told her, but I know it wasn't good. You don't get good advice from a snake.
(CLAUDIA *writes a note to* LEVINSKY.)

MACMILLAN: Mr. Kirk, did you and the defendant get along?

ARTHUR: What are you asking me? Did I ever yell at her? Sure, I yelled at her. Did I ever say, I'm tired, leave me alone? I said it, I said it more than once. But I did what I could. I did more than Bill; I tried to be a father. I took her to the plant with me; I showed her to start the ovens, I showed her how we thaw the main dishes. As soon as she was old enough, I took her in the plane with me. We had our little secrets. I've never been a girl and I don't know how they think—I know they think kind of funny—but I did right by her. By my lights, I did right.

MACMILLAN: (*Crosses Down in front of prosecutor's table then Up to Right of his chair.*) Mr. Kirk, were you surprised when your daughter's marriage collapsed?

ARTHUR: I was surprised it took so long.

MACMILLAN: You did not expect it to be a success?

ARTHUR: It was a success for him. She got to pick up his socks and he got the money. Not right away, but he knew she'd get mine. He'd show up at the house and say hello, and you could hear his head appraising the furniture. I always wondered why he never asked to see my bankbook, he was that obvious. Very polite. Please, and thank you, and how kind you are, and allow me; it was like having a goddamn headwaiter underfoot. To me, she's five feet eight inches of flesh and blood; to him, she was five feet eight inches of fresh bills.

(MACMILLAN *crosses Up Right Center.*)

Now I know I sound like your typical father, I know that; always on the lookout for fortune-hunters. But the proof is in the pudding. When he left her, he didn't leave her for a hatcheck girl. He left her for one of his clients, and she's got $10 million if she's got a dime. He started out with shad roe, had a bite of that, and decided to get a helping of caviar.

(CLAUDIA *reacts to this remark.*)

MACMILLAN: (*Crosses Left of witness stand.*) Mr. Kirk, did you engage Mr. Levinsky?

ARTHUR: No, today's the first time I've laid eyes on him. He's not a bad-looking fella.

(LEVINSKY *rises, gives* ARTHUR *a small bow. Then sits.*)

MACMILLAN: So you have no idea of his defense for your daughter?

ARTHUR: Beats me what he's doing.

MACMILLAN: Mr. Kirk, did you discuss your daughter's capacity to stand trial with anyone in the district attorney's office?

ARTHUR: Not a soul.

MACMILLAN: Mr. Kirk, do you want your daughter to get treatment?

ARTHUR: You bet.

50

MACMILLAN: (*Crosses Right and gets pad from prosecutor's table.*) And if you had the opportunity, would you pay for treatment?

ARTHUR: How much money are we talking about?

MACMILLAN: (*Crosses Up Right Center. A bit nonplussed.*) Er, that's hard to say, but—

ARTHUR: You don't have to sell me on the idea of treatment for her, but the kind of thing you're talking about can go on forever. I've got a man working for me and he's been getting treatment since 1965—his son ran off with a basketball player and he took it hard. Now to me he seems just the same as he was when he started—he still jumps when he hears a car backfire, he still yells at his wife, he still gets drunk every St. Patrick's day. I won't say he's worse. But 14 years is a long time. Do you want me to pay for treatment for 14 years?

MACMILLAN: There's no way to answer a question like that, Mr. Kirk. Would you be willing—

ARTHUR: (*Holding his hernia.*) When I had my hernia, (*Smiling,* MACMILLAN *throws pad on table and exchanges look with* ROSENTHAL.)
they took me in, they cut me open, they told me take it easy for a while and just when they said I'd be okay, I was okay.

MACMILLAN: (*Crosses Left of witness stand.*) The nature of this kind of treatment—I'm sure Dr. Rosenthal can bear me out on this—the nature of—

ARTHUR: Listen, you don't have to tell me she's sick. What she did was sick. Okay, fine. Now to me, when you're sick, you go to a doctor, and he gives you something, or he cuts something out, or he puts you on a dumb goddamn diet, and you get better. We're not talking about incurable cancer. She was sick for a few months, you're talking about paying for years.

JUDGE: Mr. Macmillan, would you like to withdraw the question?

ARTHUR: I don't mind if you keep it in. I just want to know how long I'm paying for.

MACMILLAN: (*Crosses Right of prosecutor's table.*) If your honor doesn't mind—

JUDGE: Mr. Levinsky?
(LEVINSKY *waves his assent.*)
Strike question and answer.

RECORDER: Beginning with "if you had the opportunity . . . ?"

MACMILLAN: Yes.

ARTHUR: I'll pay; not for 14 years, but I'll pay.

MACMILLAN: (*Leaning on table.*) Mr. Kirk, do you love your daughter?

ARTHUR: (*Looks at* CLAUDIA.) You bet.

MACMILLAN: Thank you, Mr. Kirk. No further questions, your honor.
(*Sits.*)

JUDGE: Mr. Levinsky?
(LEVINSKY, *with some of* CLAUDIA's *notes in hand, goes toward* ARTHUR.)

LEVINSKY: Mr. Kirk—

ARTHUR: I've been watching you; I'm ready for you.

LEVINSKY: (*Crosses Left of* CLAUDIA.) Mr. Kirk, I'm puzzled by one little thing and if we can work that out—it shouldn't take more than a minute or two—you can join your wife.

ARTHUR: I'm glad you said that because this is a hard sit, let me tell you. Sorry, your honor.

LEVINSKY: (*Crosses Left of witness stand.*) From what you've testified, you and your wife were warm, caring parents—both of you loved the defendant—

ARTHUR: You bet.

LEVINSKY: So I can't quite figure out why the defendant behaved the way you described. It doesn't make sense.

ARTHUR: It sure as hell doesn't.

LEVINSKY: Do you think you were too loving—maybe you spoiled her?

ARTHUR: Me? Not a chance. I grew up poor and I don't believe in spoiling kids.

LEVINSKY: But you did give her presents?

ARTHUR: That's not spoiling somebody. You like somebody, you give them a little something.

LEVINSKY: When?

ARTHUR: You know, like everyone: Christmas, birthdays, graduation, sometimes Thanksgiving, sometimes Easter.

LEVINSKY: Valentine's day?

ARTHUR: Oh, sure. She was my little Valentine.

LEVINSKY: And you always gave her things?

ARTHUR: When she was little I did, but I'll tell you the truth when she got older, I just gave her a gift certificate or a crisp new bill. It wasn't easy to keep thinking of the right thing.

LEVINSKY: A crisp new bill?

ARTHUR: A twenty or a fifty. Once in a while a hundred. She liked that.
(CLAUDIA *faces front—chin on hand.*)

LEVINSKY: My mother, Lily, always warned me not to give my children money.

ARTHUR: What's money? It's a piece of paper that gets you what you want. You teach your kid that, and you teach her where it comes from, and how to get it, it's a hell of a lot better than handing over something in a box with a ribbon. Tell the truth—how many presents have you gotten in your whole life that you really liked? I've got a hundred dollars that
(LEVINSKY *smiles*.)
says you've got sweaters you never wear, and ties in the bottom of your dresser, and dishes you never eat off, and I'll bet there's some godawful lazy susan sitting in the bottom of your closet. Now if I give you the cash, you could go and get yourself a movie camera or a case of Scotch. I never saw any point in giving her a nightgown if what she wanted was a bathing suit. I say, give her the money and let her choose for herself.

LEVINSKY: (*Springing the trap*.) Then why didn't you post her bail and let her choose her own lawyer?
(CLAUDIA *turns and looks at* ARTHUR.)

ARTHUR: (*Uneasy*.) Fifty thousand dollars is a lot of money.

LEVINSKY: Surely you could have put up five thousand, Mr. Kirk—a bondsman would have taken five thousand.
(ARTHUR *hesitates*.)
You do have five thousand dollars, don't you, Mr. Kirk?

ARTHUR: Yes, goddamnit, I've got five thousand dollars.

LEVINSKY: Tell me, Mr. Kirk, did you offer to post her bail? Did you?

ARTHUR: Maybe.

JUDGE: That's no answer.

ARTHUR: Yes, I offered to.

LEVINSKY: I see. And what conditions did you attach to your offer?

ARTHUR: There were no conditions.

LEVINSKY: No?

ARTHUR: We wanted to protect her; we didn't want any harm to come to her.

LEVINSKY: I see. And how did you want to protect her?

ARTHUR: (*A glance at* ROSE.) I told her we would put up the money if she came home till the trial. That's all; it wasn't much to ask.

LEVINSKY: Did you also tell her she had to use Stanley Middleton as her lawyer?

ARTHUR: No. Somebody recommended him, and I sent him over there. She didn't have to use him.

LEVINSKY: No?

ARTHUR: All she had to do was pick up the phone one time, talk to me one single goddamn time, and say, Dad, Middleton hasn't got the brains of a flea, get me Levinsky so I can come home, and I would have shipped you over there special delivery.

LEVINSKY: And then the bail money would have there, right?

ARTHUR: It wasn't a condition.

LEVINSKY: (*Crosses Right of witness stand.*) Did Mr. Middleton tell you why your step daughter discharged him?

ARTHUR: He just said she didn't like his advice—wouldn't listen to anything he told her. It's not a condition to ask your own child to come home.

LEVINSKY: After your stepdaughter discharged Mr. Middleton, did he tell you he was going to call on the district attorney?

ARTHUR: He said he was going to tell him he was fired.

LEVINSKY: That's all?

ARTHUR: I can't remember everything Middleton said.

LEVINSKY: (*Looking at* MACMILLAN.) Didn't he tell you that he planned to inform the district attorney that your stepdaughter was mentally ill and not capable of standing trial? Didn't he?

ARTHUR: (*Pause.*) Something like that.

RECORDER: I didn't get that.

ARTHUR: Something like that. He said it was the best way.

LEVINSKY: (*Crosses Down Center and Down of defendant's table to Down Left.*) I see, the best way. And when you and your wife talked to Dr. Rosenthal, when you chatted with him about your stepdaughter's behavior and about the crime she'd been charged with, did he also tell you it was the best way?

ARTHUR: Yes.

LEVINSKY: And what does that mean to you, Mr. Kirk—the best way?

ARTHUR: We're talking about a trial. A trial is a public thing, a place where you get shamed in front of the whole world. If she was your daughter, would you put her up there? Would you?
(LEVINSKY *shrugs*.)
Well, Mister Smartass, she's mine and I'm not going to let a bunch of people, a bunch of strangers, sit in a courtroom and laugh behind their hands at my baby. Oh, no. No, sir. Not while I'm breathing. You're just paid help; the day after

tomorrow, you're gone; she's the client to you, and that's all. Well, she's not the client to me. I'm not on her side just because she's giving me a fistful of money. There's 25 years of my love invested in this girl, and I'm not going to sit by and see her shamed in front of the whole goddamn world so you can earn your goddamn fee. I know your type. You find scum and you charge 'em an arm and a leg so they can walk around loose. You suck up money from other people's troubles, and you say all you're doing is giving 'em their rights under the law. I know you: whores and killers

(CLAUDIA *looks at* ARTHUR.)

are your bread and butter. Mister, no child of mine is a whore and a killer. I know what she did, and I know she wasn't in her right mind when she did it. You get that straight.

LEVINSKY: (*Crosses Left of* CLAUDIA.) So you and your wife agreed with Mr. Middleton and Dr. Rosenthal that the best way—the best way—would be to suggest to the district attorney that your stepdaughter wasn't in her right mind and wasn't capable of standing trial, right?

ARTHUR: Right, right, right!

(*He rises and crosses from witness stand to Left Center.* HARRY *rises.*)

LEVINSKY: I'm not quite through, Mr. Kirk.

(ARTHUR *looks at* LEVINSKY, *then at* JUDGE *who gestures for him to return to witness stand.* ARTHUR *slowly returns and sits.* HARRY *then sits.*)

ARTHUR: (*Arms folded.*) Ask your goddamn questions.

LEVINSKY: (*Crosses Left of his chair.*) Just one or two more, Mr. Kirk.

ARTHUR: That's what you told me before.

LEVINSKY: I'm sorry, Mr. Kirk; I'm only doing what I get paid for.

ARTHUR: (*Pulling himself together.*) You earn your money; I'll give you that.

LEVINSKY: (*Leans against his chair.*) You're very kind, Mr. Kirk. Somehow, in the middle of all that, I lost sight of what I was going after—oh
(*Crosses Left of witness stand with pad.*)
yes, I'm still puzzled by your description of your step daughter's behavior—all that distrust, all that avoiding you, all that staying away from her warm, affectionate, generous home.
(*Looking at notes.*)
Trips to your plant, flights in your plane, lots of presents, little secrets between you, all that love in the house. Maybe that was it—too *much* love?

ARTHUR: It wasn't too much.

LEVINSKY: That's right: you said you didn't spoil her.

ARTHUR: Just the opposite. She did her share; we didn't wait on her hand and foot. I raised her the way I was raised.

LEVINSKY: How do you mean, Mr. Kirk?

ARTHUR: Listen, I'm a businessman, and to me, running a home is just like running a business. You want somebody to do something, you give them something to do it. She did the dishes, she got fifty cents; putting the car away, one dollar. Even when she was little, we got some good habits started—she shined my shoes, fifty cents; she rolled my socks, fifty cents; she fed the fish—I keep guppies and angels—one dollar.
(*He laughs.*)
That got to be kinda expensive. One day, she was eight, maybe nine, she climbed on my lap and said, daddy, the fishies look awful hungry, maybe I should feed them two times a day.

LEVINSKY: So you practiced a sort of reward system with her?

ARTHUR: That's it, that's the word. I run a good business and I can tell you there are two ways to get people to do what you want: either you punish them or you reward them. People are no different than dogs—rewards work better.

LEVINSKY: Tell me, what else did you reward her for?

ARTHUR: Hmmmmmm. She used to give me a shave every once in a while; got real good at it, too. Two dollars.

LEVINSKY: A shave. That's very sweet. Anything else?

ARTHUR: No, I can't think of anything.

LEVINSKY: (*Crosses Left of* CLAUDIA, *tosses pad on table.*) Mr. Kirk, I confess you sound like a wonderfully generous father. Tell me—

ARTHUR: Hey, listen, get it straight: I love this girl. I told him that, and I was under oath when I said it. When I was courting her and she said to me, Art, what about Claudia Faith, I didn't say, send her to school, give her away. No, sir. I said, Rose, if you love her, I love her. When she woke up in the middle of the night with a bad dream, it was me, Art Kirk, who went in there and held her and sang to her. I can't sing, but I did it. I didn't know a thing about kids, but I learned. I learned what sounds she made when she was happy and what sounds she made when she was miserable. I didn't hide from the responsibility. I'm not that kind of man. It wasn't Rose and her daughter, and her husband. It was Rose and her daughter, and her father. When Rose said, Art, she needs a bath, I went upstairs and gave her a bath. Did you ever give a kid a bath? They're like puppies; they can't stay still. Jumping and splashing and getting water on everything. So your pants get wet. So what? What's a pair of pants? We had a good time. I washed her, and I dried her, and I sprinkled her all over with talcum—that's why her skin is so clear. It was so clear you could just about see through it, young skin, soft, you touched it, you felt like you were touching something magic. A child's skin is a magic thing, you know, it's got a whole feel to it you don't find in an older person. Rose taught me that: I said I can't give her a bath, and Rose said, Art, wait till you feel her skin. She was right. Listen, I'm a simple man: I loved Rose, Rose loved her, so I love her.

LEVINSKY: (*Crosses Down Left.*) And she got your pants all wet?

ARTHUR: Straight through to the skin.

LEVINSKY: (*Crosses Down of defendant's table to Right of witness stand.*) Mine does that. God, it's a mess.

ARTHUR: Listen, I'll tell you what you do. Leave 'em off, and do the job in your bathrobe. Terrycloth is best; that's what I did.

LEVINSKY: Hmmm, in a bathrobe?

ARTHUR: Terrycloth is like a towel; water won't hurt it.

LEVINSKY: I never thought of that. Of course, it doesn't stop them from splashing, does it?

ARTHUR: Nah. Nothing ever does.
(*He laughs.*)
I made faces, I sang songs—Off we go into the wild blue yonder, climbing high into the sky—she splashed and kicked, and kicked and splashed until the day I stopped giving her baths, and by that time she must have been—
(*He stops abruptly.* ROSE *is staring at him. He notices this.*)

LEVINSKY: Must have been what?

CLAUDIA: (*Turning to him.*) Aaron.

LEVINSKY: Must have been what? Sixteen years old?
(ARTHUR *looks at* CLAUDIA *who quickly turns away.*)
Is that what you were going to say?
(*Crosses Down Center and leans against railing Down Left.*)

ARTHUR: No, no, no, she wasn't sixteen. No. Come on, baby,
you know I stopped a long time before then, you know that.
Now come on, tell him the truth, you know you weren't
sixteen. You were, let's see you were—maybe—I can't remember right now—maybe—baby, you weren't sixteen. Tell
him the goddamn truth.
(*Standing.* CLAUDIA *looks down.*)
Baby— She doesn't remember; can't you see she doesn't
remember. How can you expect her to know, she's not in her
right mind, right now.

JUDGE: Take your seat, Mr. Kirk.

ARTHUR: (*To* JUDGE.) It's her word against mine, and she's not
in her right mind.

JUDGE: Sit down, Mr. Kirk.

ARTHUR: I don't like this.

JUDGE: (*Raising his voice.*) Sit down.
(ARTHUR *sits.*)

LEVINSKY: (*Left of his chair.*) Mr. Kirk—
(CLAUDIA *looks at* LEVINSKY, *then faces Right, head down.*)

ARTHUR: I'm telling you to your face I don't like this.

LEVINSKY: Mr. Kirk, didn't you stop bathing your stepdaughter the day she locked you out of the bathroom?

ARTHUR: Wait just a goddamn minute! She didn't lock me out.
I made up my own mind. I said to Rose, she's big enough to
take a bath without me, that's what I said. I said it. I told her

more than once. I didn't want to give her a goddamn bath; it was Rose's idea.

LEVINSKY: She did not lock you out of the bathroom?

ARTHUR: She locked the door. It's not the same thing. Everybody locks a bathroom door—I bet you lock your bathroom door. It's not the same goddamn thing.

LEVINSKY: I see.
(*Pausing.*)
And didn't you offer her one hundred dollars to unlock the door?

ROSE: (*Rising, stepping forward.*) Art—
(CLAUDIA *looks up at* LEVINSKY, *then at* ROSE, *then bends forward again, head down facing Right.*)

ARTHUR: It's not true. Honey, I swear it's not true, I swear on my life I never did that.
(*To* CLAUDIA.)
Baby, how could you say a thing like that? Now you just take it back; you can't say that about your daddy, that's a terrible thing to say.
(*To* CLAUDIA.)
Look at your mama, she's unhappy; take it back.
(*He stands.* HARRY *rises. Crosses Left of prosecutor's table.* HARRY *crosses Left Center.*)
Honey, I just did what you told me: I washed her—

JUDGE: Mr. Kirk.

ARTHUR: —and dried her and rubbed her with talcum. That's all.
(ROSE *turns away.*)
Nothing else, only what you told me. Baby, for your mama's sake, take it back. Now we've had a little misunderstanding, but I'm going to take care of that right now. Okay, the bail.

Daddy'll take care of that piece of business right quick.
Look—
(*Crosses Right of defendant's table taking out his checkbook and pen.*)

JUDGE: Mr. Kirk.

ARTHUR: This is daddy's magic trick—you keep your eyes on your daddy's right hand, don't take your eyes off it—five thousand dollars and no cents. Look right here, daddy's magic, five thousand dollars and no cents.
(*He rips the check from the pad and holds it before her.*)
Here you go, baby, now you take that and make your old daddy happy, you make him smile.
(*He puts the check on the table before her. She turns away.*)
Now what else? Don't tell me, I know. This fella, right? How much do you need for him?
(CLAUDIA *looks at him.*)
Come on, baby, my hand is itching and my dollars are twitching—remember that—my hand is itching and my dollars are twitching?
(ROSE *turns and looks at him.*)
Levinsky, how much? Come on, mister, you name your price right now. Right goddamn now.
(CLAUDIA *hasn't moved;* ROSE *is weeping.*)

JUDGE: Mr. Kirk—

ARTHUR: Baby, please take it back. I'm begging you, baby. Daddy is begging you.
(*Goes to his knees.*)
I'm begging you, baby. Please take it back.
(*His head is lowered, and slowly, almost unwillingly* CLAUDIA *reaches out to stroke it.*)

ROSE: (*Throwing her purse on chair.*) Don't touch him!
(CLAUDIA's *hand snaps back;* ROSE *goes to* ARTHUR, *helps him up, holds his hand, and defiantly, glares around the room.*)

LEVINSKY: I have no questions, your honor.
(ROSE *and* ARTHUR *return to their seats.* ARTHUR *lets go of her hand halfway across.* HARRY *and* LEVINSKY *sit.*)

JUDGE: Mr. Macmillan?

MACMILLAN: (*Rises.*) As I requested before, your honor, I intend to recall Dr. Rosenthal later.
(*Sits.* CLAUDIA *holds check, staring at it.*)

JUDGE: Mr. Levinsky, are you ready to proceed?

LEVINSKY: (*Rises.*) Yes, your honor.

JUDGE: Is your medical witness here?

LEVINSKY: I don't expect to call one, your honor.

JUDGE: (*Leaning forward.*) No?

LEVINSKY: No, your honor. I'm going to call the defendant.

JUDGE: Mr. Levinsky, usually in cases like this, if there's a challenge, the defense calls its own medical witness.

LEVINSKY: So I understand, your honor. I'm going to call the defendant.

JUDGE: All right. Let's take a short recess.
(*He leaves the bench; the* RECORDER *leaves her seat. Exits Right door.* HARRY *stands up Left against witness stand railing.* ROSE *and* ARTHUR *don't move.* LEVINSKY *sits.* ROSENTHAL *exits.* MACMILLAN *takes a folder. Crosses Center, back to audience reading it.*)

CLAUDIA: (*She turns back to* LEVINSKY. *Crumbles check.*) Goddamnit, Aaron!

LEVINSKY: You'll find out when you get up there that that's the way the game is played.

CLAUDIA: It's not his fault.

LEVINSKY: Fine. Whose fault is it?
(MACMILLAN *is eavesdropping*.)
Could you excuse us?
(MACMILLAN *leaves Right door*.)
It doesn't matter whose fault it is, it doesn't matter what happened. What matters is that I get what you want.

CLAUDIA: And these are your rules?

LEVINSKY: I told you that if you didn't let me bring in a psychiatrist to testify for you, it was going to get dirty. I told you. You didn't want to do it the right way, you wanted to walk in and prove you don't need a doctor, and you think doctors are shits, and you can do it on your own, fine. If you're going to tie one hand behind me, I'm going to hit harder with the one that's left.

CLAUDIA: Oh, bullshit, Aaron. You had him. You didn't have to cut him up. He's bleeding, Aaron.

LEVINSKY: Wait. You're going to be up there in a minute, and you'll have your chance to bleed.

CLAUDIA: Not me. Not your client. Don't you love your clients, Aaron?

LEVINSKY: Did you?

CLAUDIA: I'd like that cigarette now, Harry, thank you.
(CLAUDIA *throws check at him. Rises and crosses to Right door.* HARRY *follows. After a second,* LEVINSKY *picks up check and briefcase and leaves, too. When they are all gone,* ROSE *stands up and walks a few feet away from* ARTHUR, *Down Right. He looks up, rises, crosses to her.*)

ARTHUR: Honey—

ROSE: (*Not looking at him.*) Did you offer her a hundred dollars?

ARTHUR: Honey, I swear on my life, on our life together, all I did was what you told—

ROSE: Art Kirk, did you try to buy my child for one hundred dollars?
(*He is silent.*)

Blackout

Act Three

A few minutes later. As the lights come up we see that ROSE *and* ARTHUR *have managed to compose themselves and sit stiffly in their chairs.* ROSENTHAL *is back in his chair.* MACMILLAN *and* LEVINSKY *are sitting in their chairs. The* RECORDER *enters and takes her seat.* CLAUDIA *enters followed by* HARRY, *who closes the door. She looks at* MACMILLAN *for a moment, then crosses to her chair. As she does so,* LEVINSKY *rises, takes her notepad from the table and hands it to her, then hands her the pencil. They exchange smiles and sit.* HARRY *has crossed Up Left and opens the slats of the venetian blinds on all three windows. As he finishes, the* JUDGE *enters.*

HARRY: (*Standing in front of his chair.*) Remain seated please.

JUDGE: (*Sitting.*) Mr. Levinsky.

LEVINSKY: Your honor, I'd like to call the defendant, Mrs. Draper.
(*The* JUDGE *nods and* CLAUDIA *starts toward the witness stand.*)

JUDGE: You can testify from your seat, Mrs. Draper.

CLAUDIA: (*Stops. Looks at* LEVINSKY *who shakes his head "no." She then looks at the* JUDGE.) I'd like to take the stand, please.

67

JUDGE: That's all right, we'll swear you at your seat.

CLAUDIA: (*Harder.*) I'd like to take the stand, please.

JUDGE: Your testimony will be just as valid if you—

CLAUDIA: (*Crosses Center to the bench.*) It's bad enough to come in here in a bathrobe; don't make it worse. I'm a witness and I want to take the stand.
(*An edgy silence. She leans in.*)
I'm not going to hurt you, your honor. I'm really pretty harmless.

JUDGE: Of course, my dear, of course.
(*He gestures, and she goes to the stand. Looks at* LEVINSKY *making a triumphant punching gesture with arm. She has her notebook with her.* HARRY *follows with the Bible. She slaps her Left hand on it and raises the other.*)

HARRY: Do you solemnly swear that the testimony you shall give in this special proceeding shall be the truth, the whole truth and nothing but the truth?

CLAUDIA: I do.

HARRY: Be seated, please.
(CLAUDIA *sits; he sits.*)

LEVINSKY: (*Rises.*) Mrs. Draper, you are the defendant in this proceeding, right?

CLAUDIA: Yes, I'm the defendant.

LEVINSKY: Prior to your commitment to this hospital for a mental examination, were you indicted for any criminal acts in New York County?

CLAUDIA: I was indicted on a charge of manslaughter in the first degree.

LEVINSKY: How did you plead at your arraignment?

CLAUDIA: Not guilty.

LEVINSKY: And since you could not post bail, you were sent where?

CLAUDIA: The House of Detention for Women, on Riker's Island.

LEVINSKY: To wait for your trial?

CLAUDIA: Yes.

LEVINSKY: And from the House of Detention you were brought here?

CLAUDIA: Yes.

LEVINSKY: Can you tell me the names of the doctors who examined you here?

CLAUDIA: Julio Alvarez and Herbert Rosenthal. That's Rosenthal.

LEVINSKY: Did they examine you together or separately?

CLAUDIA: Separately.

LEVINSKY: How long was Dr. Alvarez' examination?

CLAUDIA: Ten minutes, maybe fifteen. He doesn't speak much English.

MACMILLAN: (*Half rising.*) Objection.
(JUDGE *holds up hand.*)

CLAUDIA: He doesn't.
(MACMILLAN *sits. To the* JUDGE.)
He's from Panama. His Spanish isn't so hot, either; the only word he seemed to know was puta.

JUDGE: Puta?

CLAUDIA: It means whore.

LEVINSKY: (*Crosses Down Left.*) How long did Dr. Rosenthal examine you?

CLAUDIA: Fifty, fifty-five minutes. He knows more English.

MACMILLAN: (*Rises.*) Your honor—
(*The* JUDGE *swallows a smile and waves him quiet.* MACMILLAN *sits.*)

LEVINSKY: Mrs. Draper, do you understand the charge against you?

CLAUDIA: Yes, I do.

LEVINSKY: Can you define it for me?

CLAUDIA: (*To* MACMILLAN.) First-degree manslaughter is a Class B felony under Section 125.20 of the Penal Law—with intent to cause serious physical injury to another person, causing the death of such person or of a third person.

LEVINSKY: What is the maximum term for first-degree manslaughter?

CLAUDIA: 25 years.

LEVINSKY: And the minimum?

CLAUDIA: It's fixed by the court.

LEVINSKY: (*Crosses Left of witness stand.*) Have you conferred with counsel concerning the charge against you?

CLAUDIA: Yes, several times.

LEVINSKY: During these conferences, did you give me all the facts and details constituting your defense to the indictment?

CLAUDIA: Yes, I did.

LEVINSKY: Did you give me the names and addresses of any witnesses?

CLAUDIA: Yes.

LEVINSKY: Did you write out for me a complete narrative of the events leading to and following your arrest?

CLAUDIA: Yes.

LEVINSKY: Did you ask me to explain to you the legal concept of justifiable force?

CLAUDIA: (*Nods to* MACMILLAN *and to* JUDGE.) ''One may use physical force upon another when—and to the extent—he reasonably believes it necessary to defend himself from what he reasonably believes to be the use—or imminent use—of unlawful physical force by such other person.''

JUDGE: (*Leaning forward.*) What does that mean to you, Mrs. Draper?

CLAUDIA: (*To* JUDGE, *tilting chair back.*) It means if somebody is working you over, and you think he's going to beat your brains through the back of your head, you can try to stop him any way you need.
(*Chair upright.*)

LEVINSKY: Did you instruct me to file a plea on your behalf?

CLAUDIA: Yes.

LEVINSKY: And what was that plea?

CLAUDIA: Not guilty.

LEVINSKY: Mrs. Draper, do you recognize the people in this courtroom?

CLAUDIA: (*Pointing as she names them.*) Judge, prosecutor, defense lawyer, court officer, recorder, witnesses. I'm the defendant, and I'm testifying in my own behalf.

LEVINSKY: Where is the courtroom?

CLAUDIA: On the seventh floor of Bellevue Hospital.
(*Smiling.*)
The morgue is right across the street.
(HARRY *looks thru blinds, nods ''yes'' to* LEVINSKY *who nods back.*)

LEVINSKY: Do you know what court it's attached to?

CLAUDIA: Special Term, Part Two of the Supreme Court of the State of New York.

LEVINSKY: Can you tell us today's business?

CLAUDIA: It's a special proceeding under Article seven-three-oh of the Criminal Procedure Law.

LEVINSKY: Mrs. Draper, can you tell us any of the provisions of Article seven-three-oh.

CLAUDIA: Sure. If I lose today, I'm committed for a year.

MACMILLAN: (*Rises.*) Your honor—

JUDGE: Let her finish, Mr. Macmillan. You'll have your cross.
(MACMILLAN *sits.*)

CLAUDIA: (*To* JUDGE.) Thank you.
(*To* MACMILLAN.) Sixty days before the year is up, the hospital can ask to retain me. If I lose again, the hospital can keep me for 2 years. From then on, the hospital can apply to hold me every two years until two-thirds of the maximum sentence on the highest charge in the indictment.
(*Pausing. Front.*)
Two-thirds of 25 years is 17 years. That's Article seven-three-oh.

MACMILLAN: (*Rises.*) Your honor—

CLAUDIA: But you guys aren't done yet.
(MACMILLAN *sits. Says this to all Stage Right.*)
If the commissioner of the hospital—this is the hospital I've been sitting in for 17 years—if he decides I'm still mentally ill and need some more treatment, he can apply to get an order of certification under Section 73 or Section 124 of the Mental Hygiene Law.

LEVINSKY: What does that mean to you, Mrs. Draper?

CLAUDIA: (*Front.*) It means, if they do it right, they can lock me up in a hospital for the criminally insane, then they can lock me up in a run-of the mill loony bin. And they don't ever have to let me have a trial. That's what it means.

MACMILLAN: (*Rises, crosses Right of bench.*) Your honor—

CLAUDIA: (*Indicating defendant's table.*) On the table over there is a book called Criminal Law. Pages 287 through 298. Look it up.

MACMILLAN: Your honor, the witness is extending the— (JUDGE *holds up hand.*)

CLAUDIA: I didn't write the book. The honorable—Eugene R. Canudo, Judge, New York City Criminal Court.

MACMILLAN: Your honor—

JUDGE: Are you questioning Judge Canudo, Mr. Macmillan?

MACMILLAN: No, your honor, but—

JUDGE: However it might be executed, that is the statute. As you should know. Proceed, Mr. Levinsky.
(MACMILLAN *crosses and sits facing front. Back to* JUDGE.)

LEVINSKY: Mrs. Draper, have you ever been admitted to a mental hospital?

CLAUDIA: Except for this one, no.

LEVINSKY: Can you recall any time you sought out a therapist—or any other mental health worker—for help or treatment or advice?

CLAUDIA: No.

LEVINSKY: Did your family doctor ever suggest to you that you undergo any form of psychiatric therapy?

CLAUDIA: No.

LEVINSKY: Did you ever not get a job, or lose a job because of the possibility of a mental illness?

CLAUDIA: No.

LEVINSKY: Have you ever been prescribed any of the drugs used to treat psychiatric disorders—anti-depressants or tranquilizers?

CLAUDIA: (*To* ROSENTHAL.) No.

LEVINSKY: Have you ever been prescribed sleeping pills?

CLAUDIA: (To JUDGE.) No.

LEVINSKY: (*Crosses Left of defendant's table.*) Do you accept the findings of the psychiatric examinations given to you here at Bellevue?

CLAUDIA: (*To* ROSENTHAL). I do not.

LEVINSKY: You reject them?

CLAUDIA: (*To* ROSENTHAL.) I reject them.

LEVINSKY: Mrs. Draper, do you believe that you're physically and mentally prepared to go on trial?

CLAUDIA: (*To* JUDGE.) Yes, I do. I believe it.

LEVINSKY: Your honor. I have no more questions.
(*He smiles; she smiles back. He returns to his seat.*)

JUDGE: Mr. Macmillan—

MACMILLAN: (*After a moment rises.*) Mrs. Draper, if you're tired, I'm sure the court will permit—

CLAUDIA: I'm not tired.

MACMILLAN: I only want to make sure you're feeling—

CLAUDIA: When I get tired, I'll let you know.

MACMILLAN: (*Crosses Up Right Center.*) Mrs. Draper—

CLAUDIA: Are you tired?

MACMILLAN: Mrs. Draper, how long were you married?

CLAUDIA: Nearly 10 years. Six weeks short of 10 years.

MACMILLAN: Was it a happy marriage?
(*She smiles, looks at* LEVINSKY.)
Was it a happy marriage, Mrs. Draper?

CLAUDIA: It had its moments. Doesn't yours?

MACMILLAN: Mrs. Draper, do you have any children?

CLAUDIA: No, no children.

MACMILLAN: Was that by choice, Mrs. Draper?

CLAUDIA: Yes, by choice.

MACMILLAN: Whose choice?

CLAUDIA: We agreed.

MACMILLAN: You jointly agreed?

CLAUDIA: He said if I got pregnant, he'd leave me. So I agreed with him. He didn't like stretch marks.

MACMILLAN: So you didn't get pregnant?

CLAUDIA: No, I did get pregnant.

MACMILLAN: You did get pregnant?

CLAUDIA: (*To* RECORDER.) January 1974.
(*To* MACMILLAN.)
We came home from a party and we were a little drunk and I couldn't put in my diaphragm. I kept putting too much jelly on it so it kept popping out of my hand.

(*Indicating with hand.*)
They do that—they're sort of like fish.

MACMILLAN: And did your husband leave you when he found out you were pregnant?

CLAUDIA: No.

MACMILLAN: So although you say he threatened to leave you, he did not leave you?

CLAUDIA: No, he was a man of honor. He took me to the abortion clinic in a taxi. A Checker; he said I'd be more comfortable in a Checker. He took me home in a Ford. I guess he figured I didn't need to be comfortable on the way home.

MACMILLAN: (*Paces Down Right and Up Right.*) Mrs. Draper, did you love your husband?

CLAUDIA: Yes, I love him. Loved him. No, I still love him.

MACMILLAN: Did he love you?

CLAUDIA: When I was properly dressed.

MACMILLAN: (*Up Right Center.*) Do you believe that's why your marriage collapsed—because you loved him more than he loved you?

CLAUDIA: No, he got a better deal.

MACMILLAN: You believe your husband left you for another woman?

CLAUDIA: I'd say he found another woman so he could leave me. But it comes out the same, doesn't it? Actually, he left long before he left. You don't get that, do you? If you leave your wife you'll send your head and your heart first. A couple of years later, your body will follow them out the door.

MACMILLAN: So when your marriage collapsed, your husband left your joint home?

CLAUDIA: No, I did. He showed me the lease with his name on it.

MACMILLAN: I see: he showed you the lease and kicked you out.
(*Makes a punching motion with his fist.*)

CLAUDIA: (*Imitating* MACMILLAN's *punch.*) Kicking wasn't his style. He liked to point.
(*Indicating with head.*)
He kept pointing to the door.

MACMILLAN: Ah. He pointed and you immediately left?

CLAUDIA: Not immediately.

MACMILLAN: Oh, you did not leave?

CLAUDIA: He had another attack of honor and moved into the St. Regis until Karen put up new wallpaper. Then he moved in with her. She puts up new wallpaper for each new man. The sheets stay the same
(*Indicates sheets by moving her hand straight across.*)
but the wallpaper changes.
(*Indicating wallpaper with hand going up.*)

MACMILLAN: Well, when did you leave, Mrs. Draper?

CLAUDIA: When he sublet it to somebody who could pay his price.

MACMILLAN: And you moved to a place you could afford— where is that, Mrs. Draper?
(*Crosses Down Right.*)

CLAUDIA: First Avenue and 55th.

MACMILLAN: Is that your present address?

CLAUDIA: Bellevue is my present address.

MACMILLAN: (*Crosses Up Right Center.*)
Is that where you were living when you were arrested?

CLAUDIA: Yes.

MACMILLAN: Mrs. Draper, did you work during your marriage?

CLAUDIA: Yes, I arranged parties.

MACMILLAN: You mean, you catered them?

CLAUDIA: No, I arranged them. I'd think of a theme and figure out how to make it work— Say, you wanted to give a party to celebrate passing the bar exam: I'd have cakes in the shape of law books, I'd have Latin phrases on the napkins and coasters, I'd have the help dressed in court clothes, I'd have a pâté molded like a gavel—do you get the idea?

MACMILLAN: And how long did you conduct this business.

CLAUDIA: Four years.

MACMILLAN: And you had a regular income from this business.

CLAUDIA: Irregular. One day I said to Peter, I'm going to get a job, I'm bored out of my mind, and he said, you give such great parties, why don't you do parties for other people? It never occurred to me to say that the last thing I wanted to do outside the house was exactly what I did in it. Ah, well live and learn.

MACMILLAN: And after you terminated this business?

CLAUDIA: I studied history. I wanted to go to law school, but Peter explained to me that the law was too complicated for me. He explained it very carefully and very slowly.
(*Slowly.*)
Darling—the—law—is—very—complicated—far too complicated—for a lovely—thing—like—you.

MACMILLAN: (*Crosses Right, then back to Up Right Center.*) When you moved into the apartment at First Avenue and 55th Street, what income did you have?

CLAUDIA: (*Glances at* LEVINSKY.) A hundred a week from Peter and $75 a week from a part-time job at NYU.

MACMILLAN: No other income?

CLAUDIA: When I signed the separation agreement, he gave me $3,500—that was about three months after I moved in.

MACMILLAN: Did you ask your parents for any money?

CLAUDIA: No.

LEVINSKY: (*Rises.*) Your honor, I don't mean to be rude but could Mr. Macmillan tell us why he's so fascinated with Mrs. Draper's finances? Is he planning to sell her a car?
(CLAUDIA *looks at* LEVINSKY.)

JUDGE: Where are you heading, Mr. Macmillan?

MACMILLAN: Your honor, I think my next series of questions will show. If you would indulge me, your honor.
(*The* JUDGE *nods.* LEVINSKY *sits.* MACMILLAN *paces Up and Down Right.*) Mrs. Draper, how long did you keep your part-time job at NYU?

CLAUDIA: About 4 months.

MACMILLAN: (*Up Right Center.*) And then you took another job, didn't you?

CLAUDIA: You're so cagy. Yes, at the Divine Body Massage Parlor.

MACMILLAN: At the Divine Body Massage Parlor?

CLAUDIA: (*To* RECORDER.) Didn't I just say that?
(RECORDER *nods.*)

MACMILLAN: What were your duties at the Divine Body Massage Parlor?

CLAUDIA: To give massages.

MACMILLAN: Are you licensed by the state of New York to give massages?

CLAUDIA: We called them body rubs; you don't need a license to give a body rub.

MACMILLAN: And that was your only duty?

CLAUDIA: (*She smiles.*) No. I had to smile.

MACMILLAN: (*Crosses Left of witness stand.*) All you did at the Divine Body Massage Parlor was give body rubs and smile?

CLAUDIA: I smoked on my breaks; I read the People's Almanac; and I tried to read about torts.

MACMILLAN: But you did nothing else for the customers of the Divine Body Massage Parlor except give them body rubs?

CLAUDIA: Not that I got paid for.

MACMILLAN: Well, what about—

LEVINSKY: (*Arm up indicating 3 with fingers.*) Your honor, the witness has answered the question 3 times.

JUDGE: Yes, I believe she has, Mr. Macmillan.

MACMILLAN: Mrs. Draper, how long did you work at the Divine Body Massage Parlor?

CLAUDIA: Five weeks.

MACMILLAN: And then, naturally, you took another job?

CLAUDIA: No.

80

MACMILLAN: I understand: you lived on what you'd earned at the Divine Body Massage Parlor, plus the $3,500 you got from your husband.

CLAUDIA: No, I spent the thirty-five hundred for furniture and kitchen stuff.

MACMILLAN: Well, Mrs. Draper, what did you live on?

CLAUDIA: (*Looks at* LEVINSKY *first.*) Gifts.

MACMILLAN: Gifts?

CLAUDIA: Uhuh.

MACMILLAN: Gifts from whom?

CLAUDIA: Friends.

MACMILLAN: Men friends?

CLAUDIA: Uhuh.

MACMILLAN: Did these men friends give you—jewelry?

CLAUDIA: Sometimes.

MACMILLAN: Furs?

CLAUDIA: I got a fox boa once.

MACMILLAN: Did they give you food?

CLAUDIA: Food? One guy used to bring caviar—is that what you mean?

MACMILLAN: Tell me, Mrs. Draper, did you exchange these jewels and furs at the supermarket? Did you offer them to your landlord?

CLAUDIA: No.

MACMILLAN: Well, how did you pay for your food—I assume you didn't live on caviar. For your rent? For your telephone answering service—you did have an answering service, did you not?

CLAUDIA: (*Rises crosses Left of* JUDGE.) Is it legal to take cash gifts?

JEDGE: I beg your pardon, my dear—

CLAUDIA: If I say to you, here's $100 just because I like you—is that legal?

JUDGE: (*Pounds bench.*) Yes, that's legal.

CLAUDIA: Thank you.
(*Also pounds bench. Then slowly crosses back to witness chair. Pauses, then looks at* MACMILLAN.)
A lot of the gifts were cash.

MACMILLAN: More than $10?

CLAUDIA: Oh, sure.

MACMILLAN: More than twenty?

CLAUDIA: Yes.

MACMILLAN: More than fifty dollars?

CLAUDIA: Yes.

MACMILLAN: (*Crosses Up Right Center.*) And these cash gifts from these men friends—these cash gifts of more than $50—were enough to pay your expenses?

CLAUDIA: Uhuh.

MACMILLAN: All your expenses?

CLAUDIA: All of them. And tuition at NYU Law School.

MACMILLAN: And what did these men expect in return for these cash gifts?

LEVINSKY: (*Rises.*) Your honor, is counsel for the People leading up to asking—

MACMILLAN: Your honor, I have not used the word "fee." (CLAUDIA *doesn't like word "fee" and looks at* JUDGE.)

LEVINSKY: The implication of—

MACMILLAN: I have not used the word "fee."

JUDGE: I'll permit an answer.
(LEVINSKY *sits.*)

MACMILLAN: What did these men expect in return for these cash gifts?

CLAUDIA: (*After a beat.*) Friendship.

MACMILLAN: What kind of friendship?

CLAUDIA: All kinds.

MACMILLAN: You talked to them?

CLAUDIA: Sure.

MACMILLAN: You listened to them?

CLAUDIA: God, yes.

MACMILLAN: You did them favors?

LEVINSKY: Your honor—
(*The* JUDGE *waves him quiet.*)

MACMILLAN: You did them favors?

CLAUDIA: Sure.

LEVINSKY: Your honor—
(JUDGE *waves him quiet.*)

MACMILLAN: What kind of favors?

LEVINSKY: (*Rising.*) I object to the implication—
(*Again the* JUDGE *waves him quiet.*)

MACMILLAN: (*Crosses Left of witness stand.*) What kind of favors did you do in return for these gifts?

LEVINSKY: (*Yelling, pounding table.*) This whole line of questioning is totally—
(JUDGE *holds his hand up again.*)

MACMILLAN: (*Yelling.*) What kind of favors?!!!
(LEVINSKY *sits, arms folded. For a second, she reels back from the force of the question. Then, looking* MACMILLAN *right in the eyes, she begins.*)

CLAUDIA: I get a hundred for a straight lay, a hundred for a hand job, a hundred for head and a hundred and fifty for rimming. An enema is a hundred alone, fifty if it's part of the session. If you want to wear my panties, that's another fifty; you take 'em home, another fifty. You come in my face, that's another hundred. No whips, no ropes, no spikes, no fists. No brown showers, no golden showers. I've got liquor and grass; anything else, you bring your own. It works like this; you call me first, we make a date, we meet for a drink, I look you over and if I like you, we make a deal. Half the cash in front, half when you leave.
(*Pause.*)
Darlin, I am worth the trouble, take my word for it. If you want the best? Do you want the best? I am not talking about some little black Alabama whore you find outside the Port Authority Bus Terminal. I am talking about a piece of ass like you have never seen. I am talking about good times, darlin, I am talking about burnin fire and colored lights, I am talking about taking your body to heaven and your mind with it, I am talking about spoiling you so bad you'll hate every other woman you touch, I am talking about cinnamon nipples that get hard when you breathe on them, I am talking about velvet

thighs that get wet when you kiss them, I am talking about my skin on your skin and my mouth on your mouth and my hair on your hair, I am talking about lovin you to death, darlin. Let me tell you, you're going to walk in hard and you're going to walk out soft, take my word for it. I am going to show you what dreams are made of, darlin, and then I'm going to give you those dreams, one by one, hand by hand, right here, just for you, all for you, nobody but you, you hear that, nobody but you. Do you get all that, darlin? Do you get what I am tellin you?
(*She looks around the courtroom.*)
Do you all get what I am tellin you?
(*To the* JUDGE.) Can he charge me?

JUDGE: Can he—er, no, he can't charge you.
(MACMILLAN *crosses slowly Up Right Center. Looks skyward mockingly, then puts his hands in his pockets.* CLAUDIA *watches him, smiling at his reaction.*)

MACMILLAN: And for how long did you do these men these favors?

CLAUDIA: One hundred and fifty-two days. Five months.

MACMILLAN: Can you tell me why you performed these favors for men for five months?

CLAUDIA: For the money.

MACMILLAN: For the money?

CLAUDIA: I made eighteen thousand dollars. Net.

MACMILLAN: At any time during these five months, did you ask your husband for money?

CLAUDIA: No, I did not.

MACMILLAN: (*Crosses Up a bit.*) Did you ask your parents?

CLAUDIA: No.

MACMILLAN: Did you believe they would have refused to lend or give you money?

CLAUDIA: They would have given it to me.

MACMILLAN: But nonetheless you preferred a life of exchanging favors for gifts?

CLAUDIA: It hurts less to sell your ass to strangers.

MACMILLAN: If you were in the same position today, would you make the same choice?

LEVINSKY: Your honor, she's not in the same position.

JUDGE: I'd like an answer.

CLAUDIA: I might.

MACMILLAN: You might once again turn to this life rather than asking your parents for money?

CLAUDIA: (*Pause.*) I don't know. Maybe if—if I thought—I don't know which price is higher—either way, you pay and you pay and—I don't know. I might.
(ROSE *lets out a small cry. Covers her face with her hands. To* ROSE.)
If you ever want to listen, Mama, I can try to explain it.

MACMILLAN: (*Crosses Down Right, Down around table to Left of witness stand.*) Mrs. Draper, earlier we learned that you took notes of your conversation with Dr. Rosenthal—

CLAUDIA: He didn't like that at all; he doesn't want anyone else to hold the pencil.

MACMILLAN: Did you take notes of your conversation with Mr. Middleton?

CLAUDIA: (*Opening steno pad. Flipping pages.*) "You're a nice girl and you don't belong here. You belong in a nice

hospital where they can help you. Wouldn't that be nice?''
He talked very nicely.

MACMILLAN: What about Dr. Alvarez?

CLAUDIA: (*Looks at notes.*) It's mostly in Spanish.

MACMILLAN: And Mr. Levinsky—did you take notes of your conversations with him?

CLAUDIA: Sure.

MACMILLAN: Mrs. Draper, did you trust Mr. Middleton?

CLAUDIA: No.

MACMILLAN: And Dr. Alvarez?

CLAUDIA: (*Putting two fingers together.*) Not from here to here.

MACMILLAN: And Dr. Rosenthal?

CLAUDIA: (*Looking at* ROSENTHAL.) Bottom of the heap.

MACMILLAN: And what about Mr. Levinsky?

CLAUDIA: (*Looking at him.*) For what he is, I trust him.
(LEVINSKY *smiles ironically.*)

MACMILLAN: And you don't trust me, do you?

CLAUDIA: Why on earth would I trust you? Are you crazy?
(*Laughs. Throws hands up.*)
Sorry. That's your question, isn't it?
(*Smiles at him.*)

MACMILLAN: Have I ever done anything to harm you, Mrs. Draper?

CLAUDIA: I don't believe this. Are you auditioning for Looney Tunes? Have you ever done anything to harm me?
(*Opening steno pad.*)

You and your buddy downtown are trying to put me away.

MACMILLAN: Mrs. Draper, you don't believe that I have no personal motive and that I'm simply doing my job.

CLAUDIA: Your job is to get me. Your job is to put me in a hospital. I don't know; I guess I'm dumb. I take that personally.

MACMILLAN: (*Crosses Right a bit.*) And naturally you believe that Dr. Rosenthal is acting out of a personal motive, don't you?

CLAUDIA: (*During this* ROSENTHAL *writes on his notepad.*) When I tell him, the food stinks, the bugs are eating me alive, and the Thorazine is killing me, he says, my dear, let's talk about where these odd feelings are coming from. Let's talk about your home.
(*She moves her chair forward so her legs stick out through rungs in railing and she leans on railing.*)
Now look at him: you can tell he's smart, can't you? Look at those glasses, look at those creases in his forehead, look at those two ballpoint pens. Smart. He went to school, he's got the papers to prove how smart he is. Now I bet you he's got a wife and kids and a nice house, and he believes in his wife and his kids and his nice house. Don't you? Terrific. But he wants me to believe in them, too. Don't you? Whores are girls who hang out on Eighth Avenue and stick needles in their arms. Whores aren't nice white girls from nice white families with nice white homes in Mount Kisco. He knows that; he knows that as sure as he knows his wife is home cleaning the oven and his kids are taking a test in school. You know that, don't you?
(*Pause.*)
But what if he's wrong? What if his wife is balling the insurance salesman and his kids are peddling angel dust in the school yard? What if he doesn't know his ass from his elbow? What if his school and his wife and his kids and his house

and his glasses and his ballpoints and his creased forehead are all bullshit? What if he's just an asshole with the power to lock me up? What if that's all he is—an asshole with power?

ROSENTHAL: (*Standing. Crosses Up Right Center to Right of bench.*) Your honor, forgive me for interrupting, but I believe the pressure of this proceeding is doing terrible harm to this patient, and she should be tranquilized and taken to the ward.

CLAUDIA: (*Hands up.*) Ah, he wants to take me downstairs.

ROSENTHAL: Your honor, I am seriously concerned for this patient's well-being—I believe she's very close to hysteria. In her paranoid way, she sees my testimony as an attack on her, and she's lashing out in retaliation. It's a typical reaction—she wants to provoke me.

CLAUDIA: All it takes to provoke him is to tell him he's not God.

ROSENTHAL: That's what I'm talking about, your honor—she's lashing out; she'll vilify me, and question my work and my life and—

CLAUDIA: The way you did mine.

ROSENTHAL: Your honor, in their paranoid way,
(CLAUDIA *starts to laugh.*)
schizophrenics are very clever and devious; they try to—you see, you see that laughter? Deliberate. That's an attempt to—listen to her—that's an attempt to provoke me. Typical schizoid behavior; classic paranoid reaction. I know this syndrome, I've seen it before.
(*Crosses Right of witness stand.*)
I know precisely what she's doing, and I know precisely how to deal with it.
(*He has moved close to the witness stand.*)

LEVINSKY: (*Rises.*) Your honor, is Dr. Rosenthal threatening the witness?

JUDGE: Doctor, take your seat, please.

ROSENTHAL: For her own sake, I insist that this patient—

JUDGE: Take your seat, please.

ROSENTHAL: This is a tactic—her whole technique is to provoke—

JUDGE: This is not N-O-2; this is my court; take your seat.
(ROSENTHAL *looks at* JUDGE, *then at* CLAUDIA *who points to his chair.* ROSENTHAL *goes back to his seat.*)

CLAUDIA: How do you think he's going to deal with me when I go back to the ward? What can he have in mind, I wonder? (*Mimics a needle in the arm.* LEVINSKY *sits.*)

MACMILLAN: (*Crosses Up Right Center.*) If you could not worry about Dr. Rosenthal for a moment—

CLAUDIA: (*To* MACMILLAN.) Sorry.
(*To* ROSENTHAL, *waves.*)
Sorry, Doc.

MACMILLAN: (*Crosses Right.*) Now, tell us, do you trust his honor, the court?

CLAUDIA: More than I trust you.

MACMILLAN: Do you trust Mr. Kirk?

CLAUDIA: No.

MACMILLAN: And what about Mrs. Kirk, your mother?

CLAUDIA: (*Front.*) My mother.

MACMILLAN: Do you trust your mother?

CLAUDIA: (*Shakes head. A pause again.*) No.

MACMILLAN: Is there anyone in this courtroom you do trust, Mrs. Draper?

CLAUDIA: (*Looks around then indicates* HARRY.) Harry.
(HARRY *is pleased and embarrassed. He squirms a bit. He and* LEVINSKY *exchange smiles.*)

MACMILLAN: Officer Haggerty?

CLAUDIA: Yes.

MACMILLAN: The only person in this room you trust is Officer Haggerty?

CLAUDIA: He can't hurt me. You can, the Judge can, Rosenthal can, they can. I don't trust people who can hurt me; not any more.

MACMILLAN: Do you believe your mother wants to hurt you?

CLAUDIA: Oh, she doesn't want to, but she will.

MACMILLAN: You don't believe she wants to help you?

CLAUDIA: Of course she wants to help me; you all want to help me—the whole damn room is nothing but a society to help Claudia. Except for Harry. Harry doesn't want to help me; he doesn't give a damn. Thank God for Harry.
(*Again* HARRY *smiles.*)

MACMILLAN: Mrs. Draper, do you believe your mother loves you?

CLAUDIA: Yes, she loves me.

MACMILLAN: Mrs. Draper, do you love your mother?

CLAUDIA: (*Pause.*) When I was a little girl, I used to say to her, I love you to the moon and down again and around the world and back again; and she used to say to me, I love you to the sun and down again and around the stars and back again. Do you remember, Mama? And I used to think, wow, I love Mama, and Mama loves me, and what can go wrong? (*Pause.*)

What went wrong, Mama? I love you and you love me, and what went wrong? You see, I know she loves me, and I know I love her, and—so what? So what? She's over there, and I'm over here, and she hates me because of the things I've done to her, and I hate her because of the things she's done to me. You stand up there asking, do you love your daughter, and they say 'yes,' and they think you've asked something real, and they think they've said something real. You think that because you toss the word love around like a frisbee we're all going to get warm and runny. No. Something happens with some people: they love you so much they stop noticing you're there because they're so busy loving you. They love you so much their love is a gun, and they keep firing it straight into your head. They love you so much you go right into a hospital. Yes, I know she loves me. Mama, I know you love me. And I know the one thing you learn when you grow up is that love is not enough. It's too much and not enough.

MACMILLAN: (*Crosses Left of witness stand.*) Let me see if I understand you correctly, Mrs. Draper. You believe that everyone in this courtroom—except Officer Haggerty—either wants to hurt you or will hurt you?

CLAUDIA: All of you can, and some of you will.

MACMILLAN: All of us can, and some of us will. Most of us?

CLAUDIA: (*Pause.*) Sure.

MACMILLAN: (*Crosses Right to behind his chair.*) I have no further questions, your honor.

HARRY: (*Rises.*) You can step down.

(*A bit confused,* CLAUDIA *begins to leave the box.*)

MACMILLAN: Your honor, I'd like to recall Dr. Rosenthal.
(ROSENTHAL *goes up, passing* CLAUDIA, *they exchange looks.*

She sits. He crosses to witness stand and sits. Crosses Up Right Center.)

Dr. Rosenthal, in view of the defendant's testimony, have you changed your opinion as to her—

CLAUDIA: Wait a second, wait one goddamn second. What is this?

JUDGE: Mrs. Draper—

CLAUDIA: (*Jumping up.*) You set me up and then you bring him back to hammer in the last nail? The hell with that. The Sixth Amendment says I have a right to a speedy and public trial. It doesn't say a thing about Rosenthal, or Bellevue, or Thorazine, or Article 730. Why me? Why not you? Did they examine you for your capacity? Did they examine Rosenthal? Did they examine them? I know a judge who jerks off under his robe, they never give him a test—

JUDGE: Mrs. Draper, you're not on the stand—

CLAUDIA: (*Crosses Up on platform to Left of* JUDGE. HARRY *rises, crosses to steps but* JUDGE *holds his hand up to stop him.*) Then take him off and put me on the goddamn stand, don't whip me with your goddamn rules. While you're playing with your rules, the meter is running out on my goddamn life. Can't you get that I understand you want to help, and I don't want your help? I know the price of your help. I know I'm supposed to be a good little girl for my mother and father, and an obedient and faithful wife to my husband,
(*Crosses Down of witness stand.*)
and stick out my tongue for the doctor, and lower my head for the judge, I know all that, I know what you expect me to do. Look, I am not just a picture in your heads. I am not just a daughter, or a wife, or a hooker, or a patient, or a defendant. Can't you get that? You don't understand the things I do, but I do have my reasons. They're not your reasons, so

they're not real to you, but they're real to me. And that's enough.

(*Crosses Down Left Center*. HARRY *moves Down a bit*.)

You think giving blow jobs for a hundred dollars is nuts? I know women who suck for a dinner and crawl through shit for a fur coat.

(*Looking at* ROSE.)

I know women who peddle their daughters to hang on to their husbands, so don't judge my blow jobs, they're sane. I knew what I was doing every goddamn minute. And I am responsible for it. I lift my skirt, I am responsible; I go down on my knees, I am responsible. If I play the part you want me to play, if I play sick, I won't be responsible. Poor, dumb, sick Claudia, she's not responsible, the poor, sick thing, she needs our help. I won't play that part. I won't give you that out. I won't be another picture in your heads, Claudia the nut; I won't be nuts for you. Do you get what I'm telling you? Goddamn you, do you get what I'm telling you?

(*She is near hysteria*. HARRY *takes a step towards her. She turns and looks at him, she stops. She wipes her mouth on her sleeve, takes a step down*.)

One more time: He can sign a piece of paper saying I'm nuts, but it's only a piece of paper and I'm not something on a piece of paper. You can't make me nuts that way, no matter how many times you sign it.

(*To her parents*.)

And no matter how many times you say it, you can't make me nuts.

(*To* JUDGE.)

Or you. Get it straight: I won't be nuts for you.

(*A silence. She turns and crosses up to the bench, leaning against it*. HARRY *crosses to Up Left Center*.)

Do you get what I'm telling you?

(*She stares at the* JUDGE, *then at* MACMILLAN, *then turns and slowly takes her seat*. HARRY *sits*.)

JUDGE: (*Pause.*) Proceed, Mr. Macmillan.

MACMILLAN: (*Crosses to Right of witness stand.*) Dr. Rosenthal, in view of the defendant's testimony, do you still believe she lacks the capacity to stand trial?

ROSENTHAL: Yes, I do.
(MACMILLAN *returns to his chair and sits.*)

JUDGE: Mr. Levinsky.
(LEVINSKY *rises.*)

CLAUDIA: (*Stopping him.*) Forget it; he won't; he can't.

LEVINSKY: (*Smiles at* CLAUDIA.) I have no questions, your honor. (*He sits.*)

HARRY: (*Rising.*) You can step down, doctor.

(ROSENTHAL *returns to his seat.* HARRY *sits.*)

JUDGE: Do you rest?

MACMILLAN: The people rest, your honor.
(*The* JUDGE *points to* LEVINSKY.)

LEVINSKY: We rest.

JUDGE: Mr. Levinsky,
(LEVINSKY *rises.*)
if the defendant would permit an examination by an independent psychiatrist, I'd consider adjourning this hearing for—14 days.

LEVINSKY: That would be—

MACMILLAN: (*Jumping up, crosses to Down Right of bench.*) Your honor, People would object. Might I point out that, for the record, the defense has rested.

JUDGE: You say People would object, Mr. Macmillan.
(LEVINSKY *sits.*)

MACMILLAN: (*Gulping a bit.*) Yes, your honor.

JUDGE: So be it.

(MACMILLAN *goes back to his chair and sits.*)

The court is concerned that the defendant has not supplied any expert medical testimony on her behalf. This is a critical flaw in the defendant's case. Nor has the defendant's behavior in this courtroom inspired the confidence of the bench.

(CLAUDIA *jumps up.*)

On the other hand, the court is not satisfied that the opinions expressed by the medical witness Rosenthal are completely persuasive.

(*He stares at* CLAUDIA *for a long moment.*)

Thus—I will remand the defendant to the custody of the Commissioner of Corrections to await trial on the felony charge of manslaughter in the first degree.

(CLAUDIA *smiles, and makes the triumphant punching motion with her arm.*)

Mr. Levinsky,

(LEVINSKY *rises.*)

I suggest you file an application immediately for reinstatement of the defendant's bail.

(*He nods to* CLAUDIA, *she bows to him. He rises and exits.* HARRY *rises and crosses to Center.* ROSENTHAL *rises, quickly says goodbye to the* KIRKS *and exits.*)

HARRY: If you have business before this court, remain seated. There will be a short recess before the next case.

(*He crosses to Right of* CLAUDIA.)

If you need matches, I've got them.

CLAUDIA: Thank you, Harry.

(HARRY *crosses and stands Up Stage of his chair.* MACMILLAN *having put his papers in his briefcase crosses Down of his table to Center and waves goodbye to* LEVINSKY. LEVINSKY *and* CLAUDIA *wave back. He then crosses Up of his table to*

the KIRKS *to say goodbye, then he exits. The* KIRKS *rise and slowly put on their coats. The* RECORDER *remains seated putting a new tape into her machine.* LEVINSKY *is putting his papers into his briefcase.* CLAUDIA *turns to him.*)
I won, goddamnit. I won.
(*He gives a pained smile and continues packing his briefcase.*)
All right, Aaron, all right. We won.
(*He throws his case on the table and pushing her chair aside goes to her and gives her a big hug. He then crosses to Left of the table and gets his briefcase.*)

LEVINSKY: (*Crossing Down of the table to Center.*) I'm going to call the office to have them prepare a bail application and ask for a trial date.

CLAUDIA: You're going to cost, aren't you, Aaron?

LEVINSKY: I've got a house in East Hampton to support. You can forget about your 18 thousand.

CLAUDIA: Now, I'm paying for your house?

LEVINSKY: (*Smiling.*) Rules of the game.
(*He waves and exits.* ROSE *and* ARTHUR *head toward the door.*)

CLAUDIA: Please—
(*They stop, turn and look at her.*)
Please—
(*A silence.*)
I'm sorry—
(CLAUDIA *takes a step forward.*)
I'm sorry for all—
(*She crosses Down Stage Left Center.*)
For all the—I'm sorry—I'm sorry I didn't accept the cigarettes. I know you went to a lot of trouble. Can I still have them? Please—
(ROSE *and* ARTHUR *look at each other;* ROSE *nods and* ARTHUR

crosses to Center and gives CLAUDIA *the carton.* ROSE *crosses Down Right.*)

Thanks, Dad.

(*She leans forward and kisses him on the cheek; she turns and crosses Down to* ROSE. *She puts out her arms and* ROSE *takes a step backward.*)

Let me touch you, Mama.

(ROSE *hesitates.*)

Mama, I love you to the moon and down again and around the world and back again. Please let me touch you, Mama— (ROSE *relents and they hug, fondly and closely.* ARTHUR *covers his eyes.* ROSE *then pulls away and exits.* ARTHUR *follows her, but when he gets to the door he turns and he and* CLAUDIA *look at each other for a moment. He then turns and exits.* CLAUDIA *bangs the carton of cigarettes against prosecutor's table, then crosses to Center where* HARRY *meets her and hands her the note pads and law book.*)

Thanks, Harry.

(*She turns and exits,* HARRY *behind her. The* RECORDER *rises and crosses Down Center.*)

RECORDER: On June 15th, 1979, Claudia Faith Draper was tried in the State Supreme Court, New York County, on a charge of manslaughter in the first degree. She was acquitted. On July 5th, 1979, Rose and Arthur Kirk filed a notice of legal separation in the State Supreme Court, Westchester County. On October 3rd, 1979, Herbert Rosenthal resigned from the staff of Bellevue Hospital and was appointed Deputy Commissioner of Mental Hygiene for the State of New York. (*She turns and exits Right door.*)

(Fadeout.)

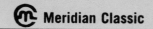
OUTSTANDING DRAMA

(0452)

☐ **FIVE PLAYS BY MICHAEL WELLER.** With unmatched intimacy and accuracy, this remarkable collection of plays captures the feelings, the dilemmas, the stances, and above all the language of the 1980's. This volume brings together for the first time five of Weller's plays, in their author's final versions. (257921—$9.95)

☐ **LORRAINE HANSBERRY, THE COLLECTED LAST PLAYS.** The three plays in this volume represent the fullest unfolding of the remarkable genius that created *A Raisin in the Sun*, and *Sidney Brustein's Window.* These plays are the lasting legacy of the extraordinarily gifted woman whom Julius Lester calls in his Foreword "the ultimate black writer for today . . . My God, how we need her." (254140—$8.95)

☐ **FENCES A Play by August Wilson.** The author of the 1984-85 Broadway season's best play, *Ma Rainey's Black Bottom,* returns with another power-ful, stunning dramatic work. "Always absorbing . . . The work's pro-tagonist—and greatest creation—is a Vesuvius of rage . . . The play's finest moments perfectly capture that inky almost imperceptibly agitated darkness just before the fences of racism, for a time, came crashing down." —Frank Rich, *The New York Times.* (260485—$6.95)

☐ **MA RAINEY'S BLACK BOTTOM, By August Wilson.** The time is 1927. The place is a run-down recording studio in Chicago where Ma Rainey, the legendary blues singer is due to arrive. What goes down in the session to come is more than music, it is a riveting portrayal of black rage . . . of racism, of the self-hate that racism breeds, and of racial exploitation. (256844—$5.95)

Prices slightly higher in Canada.

To order use coupon on last page.

PLUME

EXCITING CONTEMPORARY PLAYS

Plume

 Meridian

EXCEPTIONAL PLAYS

☐ **A RAISIN IN THE SUN by Lorraine Hansberry.** From one of the most potent voices in the American theater comes A RAISIN IN THE SUN, which touched the taproots of black American life as never before and won the New York Critics Circle Award. This Twenty-Fifth Anniversary edition also includes Hansberry's last play, THE SIGN IN SIDNEY BRUSTEIN'S WINDOW, which became a theater legend. "Changed American theater forever!"—*New York Times*   (259428—$12.95)

☐ **BLACK DRAMA ANTHOLOGY Edited by Woodie King and Ron Milner.** Here are twenty-three extraordinary and powerful plays by writers who brought a dazzling new dimension to the American theater. Includes works by Imamu Amiri Baraka (Leroi Jones), Archie Shepp, Douglas Turner Ward, Langston Hughes, Ed Bullins, Ron Zuber, and many others who gave voice to the anger, passion and pride that shaped a movement, and continue to energize the American theater today.
(009022—$6.95)

☐ **THE NORMAL HEART by Larry Kramer.** An explosive drama about our most terrifying and troubling medical crises today: the AIDS epidemic. It tells the story of very private lives caught up in the heartrending ordeal of suffering and doom—an ordeal that was largely ignored for reasons of politics and majority morality. "The most outspoken play around."—Frank Rich, *The New York Times* (257980)—$6.95)

☐ **FENCES: A Play by August Wilson.** The author of the 1984-85 Broadway season's best play, *Ma Rainey's Black Bottom,* returns with another powerful, stunning dramatic work. "Always absorbing . . . The work's protagonist—and greatest creation—is a Vesuvius of rage. . . . The play's finest moments perfectly capture that inky almost imperceptibly agitated darkness just before the fences of racism, for a time, came crashing down."—Frank Rich, *The New York Times.* (260485—$6.95)

☐ **IBSEN: The Complete Major Prose Plays, translated and with an Introduction by Rolf Fjelde.** Here are the masterpieces of a writer and thinker who blended detailed realism with a startingly bold imagination, infusing prose with poetic power, and drama with undying relevance and meaning. This collection includes *Pillars of Society, A Doll House, Ghosts, An Enemy of the People, Hedda Gabler, When We Dead Awaken,* and Ibsen's six other prose plays in chronological order.
(257972—$14.95)

Prices slightly higher in Canada.

There's an epidemic with 27 million victims. And no visible symptoms.

It's an epidemic of people who can't read.

Believe it or not, 27 million Americans are functionally illiterate, about one adult in five.

The solution to this problem is you... when you join the fight against illiteracy. So call the Coalition for Literacy at toll-free **1-800-228-8813** and volunteer.

Volunteer Against Illiteracy. The only degree you need is a degree of caring.